ReIgnited
AN ACCIDENTAL LIFE
book two

BONNIE THOMLEY

ISBN: 979-8-9898900-1-9
www.bonniethomley.com

This one is for you dad. Thanks for the laughs, good advice, and for the example you always set for me.

CHAPTER ONE

There it was again. That feeling of dread. It was a feeling that I was beginning to get used to at this point. Each time it showed up though, it got a little harder to tuck it away. A shard always remained. Quietly growing in the background. Hopefully it wasn't leading to an explosion.

As my mom always says, "this too shall pass." I sighed. Hopefully all of this would eventually. God knows I was tired of it.

Three months had passed since what I had come to call my rebirth. That day had many names, though. It was the day my brother, my ex, and my former best friend died. It was the day I became a murderer. It was the day that I played God and brought a broken man back to life. Not a day had passed that my mind hadn't been preoccupied by each of those milestones. It was something I would never be free from.

Being miles away mentally did little to make my day-to-day life any easier. Things had been so busy. After that day, Xavier and I had been filled with worry. My anxiety was at an all-time high.

The police had a lot of questions about the fire. There was nothing left of Andra. Nor was there anything left of the great people that were inside. Nothing more than ash at least. The thought of it made my chest feel heavy. For a moment, they acted like they thought Xavier committed arson, or worse, murder just to get a little insurance money. It was insulting. Who could blame them, though? It's not like we could be super straightforward about what we knew. We just hoped that our cover story would stick.

I had been a fool to think that Alex and James were the only ones that knew what was going to happen that night. Well, them and that witch of a fake friend Kate. We quickly learned that was not the case. Xavier's statement to the news was smart. The crew was working on an experiment for a better, safer flame-retardant option than what was currently on the market. Unfortunately, it was a failure and a fire got out of control.

What we didn't expect was a smear campaign, but Alex's crew got to work immediately. It appeared that before the place went down in flames, they managed to get inside. The pictures that they released looked very damning. The stories they started circulating had been wild. It was all over the internet. I was in PR overdrive. Xavier was trying hard to pretend that he was holding everything together, but he was broken. The weight of all of the deaths weighed on him heavily. He didn't bother telling me otherwise. I could see it in his eyes.

It was a heavy burden to carry. Souls that weren't ours to risk or to take. Either way, they were gone now. We would have to answer for this someday. If not to the cops, then to God himself. I still remember the feeling I felt when becoming immortal so vividly. That sinking, hopeless feeling. My true fear was that hell waited for me at the end of this all. Could I do enough good to buy my way back into heaven? I hoped so.

I had to chuckle at myself for a moment. Heaven. The blackness that I experienced the day that I changed… deep down I knew what it was. It was my soul cutting ties with me. Now I was just a shell. What else could it be? I needed to start being realistic. I couldn't bring myself to talk to Xavier about it. I didn't want to add to his plate. Truth be told, I didn't want to speak it into existence either. For now, it would have to be my burden to bear alone. I was getting used to it. After all, stress and I were definitely not strangers anymore.

CHAPTER TWO

"The check from the insurance company arrived today." Xavier said solemnly as he appeared in the doorway of my office.

"Have you made your decision, then?" I knew he hadn't. I was just trying to be a part of the conversation. He didn't have to say much about it. I could feel the vibes he was putting off. It was confusion.

"I don't know." Xavier said as he entered the room, closing the door behind him and sitting down across from me. "My mind is all over the place.

There are pros and cons to each decision, and I can't put my finger on which outweighs the other." His hair was disheveled.

He sighed and I got up from my chair. I walked over to Xavier, sat down on his lap, and laid my head on his. I knew how much all of this was weighing on him. Even if we weren't together, it would be apparent. The dark circles around his eyes, his slightly disheveled appearance. If anyone had a suspicion that he was immortal, they would change their minds when they laid eyes on him.

"Typical Libra. Always weighing out the options." I chuckled. "I wish I knew what to tell you, sweetheart. I really do. I know that this is all taking a toll on you. You can try to hide it all you want, but I know you."

"Amy, I wish your father was here right now. He would know what to do and I would trust his opinion. When I needed advice, especially in my early days, he was the one I went to."

"That makes two of us. He always seemed to know what the right moves were. Mom used to joke that he had infinite wisdom. He would try to act humble about it, but he knew that she was right."

Xavier kissed my forehead as I moved to stand up. I returned to my office chair and grabbed a notebook.

"Let's do this together. What are the pros of rebuilding Andra?"

"Well, all of our immortality research relied on Andra. Our research can't really continue at Nectar. There are too many eyes on us here."

"And the cons?"

"Suspicion. This smear campaign might make it hard to continue anything there at all. You have done a fantastic job spinning all of the stories in the press, but will it be enough? It will also be costly. We could use the insurance money for more important things."

"I wish I could promise that it will be enough. It's hard to know what Alex's group might still be sitting on. It would be over. They could also be holding back until we make a move. Who knows what they might have?"

"I feel like rebuilding is such a big risk. We still have all of the research information in the safe. If we wanted to or needed to use it in the future… well, we will still have it all. We can always make more serum. Plus, we have a few vials on standby."

"It sounds like you are leaning toward not rebuilding." I was torn. Part of me would be happy to not have the burden of rebuilding but the other part thought it might be a good project to occupy Xavier.

"Yeah. Saying it all out loud has given me a little more clarity. What do you think about it? You have a say also. This might be my company, but the immortality affair affects you just as much as it does me. This is ours."

"Xavier, I support you no matter what choice you make. We are in this together."

"Let's just try to move on with our lives then. Our lives might be a lot different now, but that doesn't mean that we can't live normally. They will just last a bit longer than everyone else's."

"There is one thing, though." I sighed, knowing that this decision would impact more than just us. "You have to break the news to Martin."

"Yes, that won't be easy. He could have died at Andra that night. By all means, he should have been there. He wants to see it through. Hopefully he will be able to see that this is all for the best."

Xavier was right. Martin was supposed to be at Andra when it went up in flames. That was the deal. Xavier would take the day shift and Martin the night shift. That's not what happened that night, though. When it was time for him to leave, he went outside to discover that he had a flat tire. He was probably pissed at the time, but it saved his life at the end of the day. Hindsight was always 20/20 I suppose.

Was it a miracle? Perhaps. It was definitely

convenient and honestly, a bit suspicious. Maybe I was just becoming jaded after a rough couple of years. I wanted to get Xavier's take on it, but he had a lot on his mind.

"Stop, Amy."

"What?" I looked up, startled. His voice sounded harsh.

"Stop acting like you can't talk to me. Yes, I have a lot on my mind. You do too and I can tell. I am not as sensitive as you apparently think I am."

"I don't think you are sensitive. I think you are overwhelmed. Why would I add to your plate?"

"Because we are a couple. Because that's how relationships work. Because you are supposed to trust me."

"I do trust you, Xavier."

"Then say what you are thinking."

I was quiet for a moment. What was I thinking? There was more going on in my brain than he could even imagine. As I started to mentally go through the catalog of nonsense I had acquired in my brain, I began to lose it. It was too much.

"Where do you want me to start? Let's see… In the last couple of years, my dad was murdered by my brother and boyfriend. Both of whom are dead now. One at my own hands. Martin somehow managed not to be there and that is beginning to seem awfully convenient. Oh, also… when I became immortal, I had a black, sinking feeling as I fell through a void. I can only assume that feeling was my soul leaving my body. Every night I go to bed worried that I am some sort of monster bound for hell if the day ever comes that I actually do die somehow."

Hot tears were streaming down my cheeks. It had all come to a head. Xavier was quiet for a moment as he mentally processed everything that I had just unloaded on him. I felt bad. It wasn't intentional. Once I started, I just couldn't stop.

"Just talk to me about these things, Amy. You want to shield me from it but if you had just spoken up, you would have found out that I have had every single one of those thoughts in my head too. The suspicions of Martin. The empty hollowness that is in my body… well I think about it every day too."

I should have known.

"You're right. I should have spoken up earlier."

"Better late than never." He winked at me as he wiped the tear remnants off of my cheeks. "Let's go give Martin our news and feel him out a bit."

I nodded and gave him a quick kiss before we made our way out.

CHAPTER THREE

Xavier and I were nervous about delivering the news about not rebuilding to Martin. Even if we were a little leery of him right now, he was still our friend. Our suspicions could be completely off base. We decided it would be best to tell him in person. He had been working from home since the fire. Xavier knew that he felt responsible. If he had only been there as planned, maybe everyone would still be alive.

"Is that my mom's car in the driveway?" I asked out loud as we approached Martin's house.

"It looks like it, but why? Have they ever met each other?"

"Only once that I know of."

I quickly unbuckled and hopped out of the passenger seat. I was eager to get a closer look at the car. It definitely belonged to my mom. That familiar window decal made it hard to mistake. A small pair of angel wings enveloped in an infinity symbol. She had gotten it shortly after becoming a widow. She said it represented her eternal love for my father, even in death.

Xavier quickly made it to my side and linked arms with me. He ushered me to the front door, equally anxious for some answers. He rang the doorbell, and I fidgeted as we waited.

"Just stay calm." He whispered to me right before the front door began to open.

"Good evening, Xavier, Amy. Come in. To what do I owe the pleasure?" Martin greeted us and motioned for us to enter the house.

"Martin, is my mom here?" I blurted out as Martin was closing the door behind us.

Martin hesitated but eventually nodded his head.

"But why?"

"I think it would be best if we discuss this with

her. Follow me. She is in the living room.”

Xavier and I exchanged a curious look and followed Martin. As promised, my mom was sitting on the couch in the living room.

“Hi, honey.” She greeted me with a smile as if this was normal. “I wasn’t expecting to see you this evening.”

“What are you doing here mom?” I didn’t waste time exchanging any kind of formalities. I wanted answers. Maybe I was extra paranoid these days, but I didn’t care.

“Well, this obviously isn’t how I wanted you to find out about Martin and me.”

“Martin and me? You guys are together? Romantically?”

“Yes, we are. I wanted to tell you honey, but you have had so much going on. I didn’t want to add to your plate.” That sounded familiar.

“How did you two even meet?”

“Well, I have actually known Martin for quite a while. He knew your father just like Xavier. After he passed, we kept in touch. Eventually, this just happened.”

“Why didn’t you ever mention this to me, Martin?”

“It wasn’t intentional. The timing was never

right. In the beginning, I didn't want you to think your success at Nectar was because of your father. You needed to earn that yourself and know that your merits were your own. After that happened, well, so many other things were already going on."

I didn't speak for a moment. Taking all of it in was a bit much and I didn't know how I felt about all of it. It wasn't up to me anyway.

"We weren't trying to hide it, Amy." My mom said softly. "I hope you can be okay with this. I know it is probably hard to think of me with someone other than your father. It was bound to happen at some point. I can't stay alone forever."

She was right. I hated the thought of someone else swooping in and trying to take my dad's place. She couldn't be expected to live alone for the rest of her life. She was still young. She deserved the joy.

"All I care about is your happiness, mom. If Martin brings that, then I am very happy for you. Is it weird? Yes. It will take a while for me to adjust. I'll try not to make it weird." I said as I reached down and gave her a hug. She chuckled.

"Now that this is all behind us, do you want to tell me why the two of you stopped by? I think I can safely assume it wasn't to interrupt a date night." Martin seemed skeptical.

"Of course not. Why don't we all sit down."

Xavier suggested. Martin nodded.

We each took a seat. Mom and Martin each in a recliner. Xavier and I on the couch. I put my hand on Xavier's knee. I knew he was nervous. He didn't want to hurt his friend.

"We got the insurance check today. As you know, I have been going back and forth trying to figure out what to do exactly. I have had so many sleepless nights thinking things over. It has consumed me."

"Yes, I do know that. Have you made your decision? I'm now assuming that is what you are here to tell me." Martin was trying not to sound defensive, but it wasn't working as well as he probably hoped. "Your decision that it."

"I have. I think it would be best not to re-pursue our endeavors at Andra at this point in time. There are too many variables to safely conduct our research. We don't know what our enemy is keeping in their arsenal. There is a lot that can be done with the insurance money. I think investing it in research is the best decision."

"While this isn't the decision I was hoping for, I do understand the logic behind it. It would have been bittersweet to rebuild and return. Part of me feels like I owe it to everyone who died that night. I should have been there with them. Who knew a dead battery would end up being such a blessing? I appreciate you coming here to tell me in person, Xavier."

They shook hands and I anxiously waited until enough time had passed so that leaving wouldn't seem rude. I hoped Xavier caught what I just had. The biggest red flag that Martin could have flown.

"We should leave you two to your evening. Mom, call me tomorrow so we can talk a little more. I love you."

"I love you too, sweetie. Text me when you get home so I know that you made it safely. Let's have brunch on Sunday."

"Brunch sounds great. Good night."

Xavier gave a quick wave, and we headed back to the car.

I exhaled deeply the second we were outside. Why did everything in my life have to be so complicated?

"You handled that well."

I gave Xavier a half smile at the compliment. He meant well and I suppose someone had to address the elephant in the room.

"Thanks. I'm getting pretty good at thinking on my toes these days."

"Agreed."

"Did you catch what Martin said before we left?" I asked the second I closed the car door. I didn't want to risk saying it before and having a surveillance camera picking it up. I didn't know what kind of camera system Martin might have protecting his home."

"The dead battery? Yes. I heard it too."

"What do you think?"

"I think he is obviously lying. Why? That I'm not too sure about. It could be as simple as a person wanting to play hooky from work. It could be something much more serious."

"I don't like it. And now mom is involved. I don't want her to end up in the middle of anything. You don't think he started the fire, do you?"

Xavier hesitated for a moment.

"No. I don't think he would do something like that. He couldn't have killed all of those people. They were people that he knew. Some of them for years. Only a monster could do that."

CHAPTER FOUR

The rest of the drive back to Xavier's house was quiet. I had so many things going on in my mind. Mom and Martin? I wanted her to be happy, but it was still weird. The shenanigans with Martin made it even more complicated. My brain was jumping from one conclusion to another. When Xavier finally spoke, I jumped so high that I don't know how my head didn't touch the ceiling.

"It's Wednesday. Does that mean that you are staying at your place tonight?"

"Yeah. I was planning on it."

It had become my Wednesday ritual. I would go back to my house, clean a bit, make a cup of tea and soak in the bathtub. If I was feeling a little extra, I would light a candle and throw a bath bomb into the mix. It was silly, but I enjoyed my routine. With so much turbulence around me, I needed the constant.

Xavier parked his car in the driveway and made it around to my door before my hand even made it to the handle. He helped me out of the car, and I took a minute to stretch. He was such a gentleman.

"You know... you don't have to go. I don't need a break from you." He wrapped his arms around my waist.

"It's not about having a break from each other. Even though I'm not there much, I still need to tidy up and just be there enough. Vacant, unused homes always end up falling apart. I don't want that to happen to mine."

"I get it. Do you want me to drop you off and pick you up for work in the morning?" He kissed me on the cheek, and I giggled as I squirmed away.

"No, I don't want to add it to your plate. Mornings are rough enough."

We both laughed at the truth of that statement. Even though we were immortal, we still struggled in the morning like we did when we were mortal. I guess some things never change.

I grabbed the keys out of my purse and headed in the direction of the front door.

"You're leaving already?" He sounded disappointed. It made me feel a bit guilty.

"Yeah. I'm a bit tired and I have a lot on my mind. I didn't even know my mom was dating again let alone dating Martin."

"Well then, I will see you in the morning." He wrapped his arms around me and kissed the top of my head.

I lingered there for a moment with my arms around him. It was hard to let go. This had become my safe place. My constant. I knew that he was right. He wouldn't care if I stopped going to my own house each week. The independence that it made me feel was important, though.

"I'm just a phone call away, Amy. You can always come back in the middle of the night." Xavier reminded me as our hug broke.

"I'll call you before I go to bed tonight."

"Looking forward to it. Maybe you can tell me a sexy bedtime story."

I laughed as I got into the car. He stood in the driveway, watching me drive away until he could no longer see me.

Normally, I would turn the radio on and blast pop songs from the 90's. Not today. Today, I just needed to think. It had been a busy day. We were officially not rebuilding Andra. My mom was dating again, and Martin at that. Don't get me wrong, I thought Martin was a great guy. Until recently, at least. He looked out for me when I was the new girl at Nectar Corp, trying to prove herself and solve a murder all at the same time. I knew that I could always go to him if I needed help. Those facts didn't make it any less weird, though.

By the time I pulled into my driveway, I had to blink. I had been so deep in thought during my drive, I didn't remember most of it. I reached over and clicked the button to open the garage. I pulled in, closed the garage door behind me, and turned off the ignition. The garage was quiet, and I sat in my car for a moment, just soaking it in.

I walked through the garage into the kitchen and dropped my purse onto the counter. I knew I needed to clean up a bit, but I really was tired. I sighed and closed my eyes while slowly moving my neck side to side, trying to stretch.

"Bet you thought you'd never see me again, didn't you?"

A voice came from behind and before I could even turn around, someone was on me. One arm wrapped around my arms, pinning me into place. I gasped as a hand went over my nose and mouth. His body was pressed hard up against me. Something about it felt familiar. There was a strange smell. Somehow, I detected that before I noticed that there was a rag in the person's hand.

I tried to fight back, but I was fading fast. My movements were slowing, my eyes were becoming heavy. Why was this happening? Who was this?

Darkness.

When I awoke, I was completely disoriented. I tried to move but I couldn't. As I gained clarity, I realized that my hands and feet were bound. I was sitting in a chair. I wanted to look around and try to get some answers, but I was frightened. Fear was going to get me nowhere fast. I had to be brave. As I finally got the nerve to peer around, I was only met with more questions. None of this looked familiar.

I heard someone in the room moving around, but nothing could have prepared me for who came into view.

"Surprised to see me baby?"

No. This had to be a dream. Well, technically this would be some kind of nightmare. It couldn't be real, could it?

"How is this possible? I saw you die."

"No, you saw me get shot. You made the assumption that I died. You never came back to check on me, baby."

He was right. I never considered the fact that Alex might be alive. James was so close when he shot him. How did he survive?

"Where are we? What do you want from me?"

"Somewhere no one is going to find us. And as for what I want from you, that is a bit more complicated. I know that Professor X made the immortality serum. All I want is the antidote. Well, that and everything regarding the immortality serum to be destroyed. The product, the research, any experiments that might be lurking around, all of it."

"There isn't an antidote, Alex."

"Well then it looks like Prince Charming has some work to do."

"You don't get it." I cried out, becoming increasingly frustrated. "Andra is gone. There is no safe place to do this. After all of the shit your group leaked to the press, there are eyes everywhere."

"I don't see how that's my problem. Either he figures it out or you die. It's really simple, sweetheart."

He didn't know that I was immortal. I thought

that he would have figured it out already. Hopefully this would give me an advantage. As long as Xavier didn't spill the beans prematurely.

"Do you want me to call Xavier then?"

"Nah. I think I'll let him sweat a little first. He will notice you are missing soon enough. He sent you a text earlier. I took the liberty of replying to let him know that you were just too sleepy for that bedtime story he was hoping for."

What. The. Hell.

"How the hell did you unlock my phone?"

"You're quite predictable, Amy. Your dad's birthday? Please. A child could crack that code. You know for a smart girl; you make stupid mistakes."

He did nothing to mask the harshness in his words. I meant nothing to him anymore and he wasn't going to tip toe around that fact. Who was I kidding though? He probably never cared in the first place. I was nothing more than a chess piece to him.

"I say for now, we both get some sleep. I can't trust you to just sit here all night and not get into trouble. Want to share the bed with me like old times?"

"Fuck you, Alex." I spit in his direction.

"I thought that might be your answer. In that case, I'm gonna have to give you a little something to knock you out. Have it your way."

I tried to struggle but it was useless. I was tied too tightly. He plunged a needle into my arm and grinned.

"Sleep well baby." He whispered in my ear as I slowly lost consciousness.

CHAPTER FIVE

"Rise and shine." Alex shouted as he turned the lights on.

I woke up confused. Where was I? Reality came flooding into me once I looked around. I was Alex's prisoner.

"Twelve missed calls and twenty three text messages. He's talking about calling the police, so I figured we would go ahead and get this show on the road. I'm going to call him back. You are to say *nothing* until I direct you to do so. I think I'll put it on speaker phone. That way if he leaves you hanging, you get to hear it with your own ears."

Alex pulled out my phone, punched in my password (still baffled by how he remembered my father's birthday), and began to call Xavier. It only rang once before he picked it up.

"Amy, what the fuck?" His voice was angry, panicked, desperate.

"No, I wish. I tried to get her to sleep in the bed with me last night, but she wasn't having it. Such a prude. I wanted to take a long stroll down memory lane if you catch my drift."

Brief silence hung in the air. Xavier was trying to figure out who he was talking to.

"Alex?"

"You caught on quicker than I thought. Amy seemed to think she was talking to an actual ghost in the beginning. Kudos for being sharper than her."

"What have you done with her?"

"Relax X. I haven't hurt her. Not really. I need something from you, and I know you won't cooperate if I hurt your little plaything, charity case, flavor of the month, experiment… whatever you are calling her these days."

"Prove to me that she is okay."

Alex motioned to me to start talking.

"I'm okay Xavier. He hasn't hurt me."

I wanted to say more. I wanted to tell him that I had been kidnapped and drugged, but I knew Alex would retaliate somehow.

"There you have it. She's fine. Now are you ready to talk?"

"What do you want from me dude?"

"I want the antidote."

"There is no antidote."

"Don't play with me Xavier. Why would you create the technology to make someone immortal and not also make an antidote for it?"

"Because you burned down my building before I had the chance to, Alex! You think I built an entire lab in the woods just to finish the serum? I was already almost done with it when we started building. I had bigger plans in store before you came along and ruined everything."

"Be that as it may or may not be, I still want an antidote. If I don't get it, along with the destruction of any remaining serum, research, and any immortal experiments you have walking around, Amy dies. Your excuses don't mean shit to me."

"I will do anything you want. Just don't hurt her."

"Call me back when you have something

figured out."

Alex hung up the phone and I fought back tears. I knew last night that this was a bad situation, but the reality of how much my life hung in the balance was really starting to hit me. I might be immortal, but Alex didn't know that. My body might be built to survive, but that didn't mean that I was safe from pain and torture. It didn't mean that my body wouldn't eventually give out. Alex would figure out what I was long before that happened, though. Hopefully Xavier figured out that Alex was in the dark about that after he made his threat about killing me.

Alex laughed as he left the room. I didn't know where he was going or what he was going to do. He didn't say a word. That was fine with me. Being in his presence was hard. I felt so emotional. Yesterday I thought he was dead. Now he had me tied to a kitchen chair like some sort of animal.

Sitting in this wooden chair was a drag. It was uncomfortable. The ropes were too tight, and I didn't have much room to shift my weight around. If I moved too much, my wrists would start to feel burned. My lower back was killing me. How long was he going to leave me like this?

What a jerk.

It was hard not to sit and think about the times

that we spent together. There had been so many laughs and so much love. I shuddered at the thought of being intimate with him. Before it made me feel like I was on cloud nine. Now it just made me feel dirty.

Hours ticked by and I didn't see Alex. I could hear noises in the house, so I knew that he was still here. My stomach was growling. I needed to pee. The whole situation made me just want to cry. I thought about calling out to Alex to see if he would let me go to the bathroom. Surely he didn't expect me to hold it. I decided to wait and see what happened.

I eventually heard a door open and said a quick prayer for some relief. Alex walked into the kitchen. I was going to avoid eye contact but decided against it. All I could do was hope and try to appeal to his human side. He had to have a bit of one.

"I probably need to feed you while you are here. Are you hungry?"

I nodded.

"I'm still not much of a cook, but I will make us some sandwiches."

"I need to go to the bathroom. You don't expect me to hold it this entire time do you?"

"No. I expect you to piss all over the kitchen."

I didn't know if he was kidding or not. Either way, I wasn't in the mood for his bad jokes.

"I'll untie you. Don't try to pull any shit."

I agreed. I couldn't make that promise forever, but I knew that now wasn't the time. I was probably fast enough to get away. It was too risky, though. I didn't know who else was involved. I didn't even know where I was right now.

After he had me untied, he kept a tight hold around my arm as we walked to the bathroom. When he closed the bathroom door behind us and didn't leave first, my heart sank.

"You're staying in here?"

"It's nothing I haven't seen before." He chuckled before turning around to face the door. "Easy. I'm not gonna watch you. Besides, if you have to go bad enough it shouldn't be a problem. Even with a shy bladder."

I sat down begrudgingly. There wasn't time to argue. He was right. I needed to go, and his presence wasn't going to stop it from happening.

"Guess I forgot to ask if you only needed to go number one or not."

"You don't have to be such an asshole. You know that right? I am being held captive regardless of your attitude. Being like this serves no purpose."

"What a dumb thing to say. Did you forget the day we broke up? Did you forget *why* we broke up? So yeah, I feel like my attitude is perfectly justified, Amy."

That one hurt. Even if I didn't think it was true. To him I was a chess piece. He was never going to stick around. I quickly pulled my pants up and flushed the toilet before he could say anything else.

"I'm done."

He turned around and looked at me before grasping my arm again. He opened the door and escorted me back to my chair in the kitchen.

"I don't feel like feeding you, so I'm going to tie up your legs and waist. Your hands will be free until you are done eating. If you mess this up, I won't be feeding you again."

I said nothing. He quickly tied me up like he said and made our food. When he was finished, he placed the sandwich on the table beside me. As I began to eat, he sat across the table facing me. We ate in silence, and I was thankful for that. His mouth was making this situation worse. Once we were finished, he let me chug some water. The second I was done he tied my arms back up and disappeared again.

Thank God.

CHAPTER SIX

"I hope your boy toy calls soon. I'm getting tired of waiting." Alex snorted as he looked at his watch.

"Why do you hate him so much?"

"You know why, Amy. He is an evil piece of trash. Who knows what kind of abominations he has roaming around that no one even knows about."

It was hard not to chuckle. If he only knew what I was. Immortal maybe, but certainly not an abomination. He'd never see it that way.

"You're wrong about him. He's not what you think he is, and neither is his immortality project."

"He's brainwashed you. I was afraid that would happen if you went to work for him. I will admit, though, I thought it would take longer for you to start drinking the Kool-Aid. I thought it would take a bit longer for you to start sleeping with your boss too, but here we are."

I just shook my head. What a jerk. He was wrong, but I wouldn't be able to convince him. His mind had been made up about Xavier for a long time. There was nothing I could say right now that would change anything.

"If you are so convinced that there is nothing wrong with immortality and that it doesn't turn someone into a monster, you need to prove it to me. We both know that you have no way to do it. Isn't that right? Just chatter. You're trying to defend someone who isn't worth defending."

"Immortality won't turn someone into a monster. Stop saying that."

"How can you be so certain, Amy? What makes you think that you would even be able *to* know something like that?"

My heart was racing. I was either on the brink of a breakthrough or my own downfall. Should I tell him? It could give me the upper hand. It could end horribly. I was already his prisoner. What did I really have to lose? My soul was already lost. It doesn't get much worse than that.

"Because that night at Andra… After James shot you, I ran. But I wasn't fast enough. When I was trying to get away, he shot me. I floated down river, desperately holding onto consciousness. I was almost dead by the time I made it to Xavier. He saved me the only way anyone could at that point. He injected me with the immortality serum. It brought me back to life."

Alex just stared at me, trying to decipher if I was telling the truth or not. It was quite the story. I could try to play it off if I needed to. The damage was probably already done.

Telling him could have been a mistake. What if he wanted proof? Would he hurt me just to find out if I was being truthful? As the truth spilled from my lips, I hadn't even thought of that. Now that he was staring into my eyes, a desperate fear showing in his own, I realized I probably said too much. I was all in now, though.

"Do I look like a monster to you, Alex? Or do I just look like a girl who once loved you so deeply that it made her a big enough fool to believe that love was mutual?" My breath hitched unexpectedly, and I had to swallow a lump in my throat. I hated feeling this vulnerable.

Alex stood up from where he was sitting across from me in the kitchen. He turned his back and walked to the sink, turning it on and running his hands under the stream of water. He turned the knob off and rubbed his wet hands on his face and through his hair. He sighed as he turned back around.

"Is that what you really think? You think I didn't love you?"

I just told him that I was immortal and that's what he asks me?

"How could you? You helped my brother kill my father. You held me as I cried so many times, knowing that you were the one that caused the pain I was feeling. Then, when you were frightened that I would uncover the truth, you split. For so long, I thought that you really did leave because your hate for Xavier was stronger than your love for me. While that might be true, it's not the reason that you left. Fear drove you away. If you had loved me at all, things could have been different."

"For a smart girl, Amy, you can be so naive. Yes, I hold half of the responsibility for what happened to your dad. But don't be a big enough fool to think that the plan was my brainchild. Your brother was my friend. He was my right-hand man.

When he told me that your father was going to help Xavier create an army of immortal soldiers, I had to help him. By the time he came to me about everything, he already had a plan. I just helped him carry it out."

"Well, if you had been able to pull your head out of your own ass for just a moment and did your own research, you would have discovered that James was feeding you fables. Perhaps you are the one suffering from a case of severe naivety."

Alex scoffed before opening his mouth to say something. His phone rang before any words slipped past his lips.

"You have my antidote yet?" Alex said with a rather casual tone.

Before Xavier even had a chance to say anything my heart began to race. A hundred different scenarios seemed to play in my head at once. I needed him so badly.

"I want to talk to Amy before I tell you anything. And not like last time."

Alex put the phone in front of me with only a slight bit of hesitation.

"I'm still ok, Xavier." I exhaled into the phone. I had so many things that I wanted to say in that moment, but I could barely get any words out.

"This is almost over. You just need to hold on a little longer, angel. Okay?"

"Yeah. I can do that."

Alex took the phone away. I wanted to cry, but I held it in.

"Alright. You know she's good. What about my antidote?"

"Be ready tomorrow. Martin will meet you. I expect you to have Amy there with you. She is to leave with Martin. Agreed?"

"Yeah. I mean, I think it's a bitch move not to come yourself, but I get it. You're scared. Call me tomorrow with the location."

Alex hung up before Xavier could say anything else. I was relieved to know that I would be getting out of here tomorrow. I couldn't shake Alex's words, though. Why wasn't Xavier coming to get me himself? Alex laughed and it snapped me out of my thoughts.

"What's so funny?"

"You. This strong independent woman dating a coward. Think about it. If he wasn't, he would be coming to get you himself. Instead, he is sending Martin."

"Whatever, Alex. Nothing I say about it will matter to you anyway."

"You might be right. Then again, you might have it all wrong. Like I was about to say before your boyfriend's call interrupted us, you don't know as much as you think you do."

"Yeah? Well, neither do you."

He sneered as he turned and left the kitchen.

CHAPTER SEVEN

I tried to stretch, but having my arms tied made it difficult. He only untied me to go to the bathroom. It was humiliating. He wouldn't let me be in the bathroom alone. I don't know how he thought I would be able to escape that easily. Nevertheless, I was trying to limit the bathroom breaks as much as possible.

I quietly strained my ears to see if I could hear Alex anywhere nearby. If he was there, he wasn't making it easily known.

"Are you in there?" I called out, unsure of

where he went when he left the room.

Silence. I was going to ask again but I hesitated. I could hear light shuffling in the other room.

"Yeah." Alex sighed. "Still here. What's up?"

"I was hoping to make a small truce."

After another moment of silence, he appeared in the entryway.

"Oh yeah?" He looked surprised as he ran his fingers through the top of his hair. "What are your terms?"

"I give you my absolute word that I won't use it as an opportunity to escape… and you let me go to the bathroom alone."

He turned away from me, and I instantly felt defeated. If he had any love for me at all, I thought, sure he would meet me in the middle with this one. Now he was just going to walk away.

"Don't make me regret this, kitty cat." He said calmly as he opened a drawer and grabbed a pair of scissors. I shuddered at hearing the nickname he gave me when we were dating. I stifled a gasp. I really expected to have to put up a little fight at least.

Instead of him releasing me from behind where I was bound, he stood in front of me. He hesitated before leaning down, reaching his arms around me on either side of my waist.

"I meant what I said earlier. It's not a game." He whispered in my ear before I felt the rope fall away.

I stretched my arms out as Alex backed away from me. I slowly stood up, my legs feeling numb and slightly painful.

"I know you're uncomfortable. I'm sorry. Do you want me to walk with you?"

"I got it." I said coldly.

"There's shower stuff in there if you want to shower. I can give you a shirt and some shorts to wear." His voice followed behind me.

As much as I hated to admit it, I needed to shower. Hopefully this wasn't a trap.

"Alone?"

"Yes." He laughed. "Alone."

I nodded and waited in the bathroom while he went to get clothes. When he returned, I grabbed the outfit and locked the door behind him.

I slowly made my way to the toilet and sat down. It was so relieving to just sit down untied and alone.

The water was hot when I stuck the first foot in the shower. I eased the rest of the way in and just stood there. Motionless. I wanted to cry as I washed all of the negativity away, but I had to be stronger than that.

It felt like I was in the shower for hours. Realistically, it was closer to 20 minutes. After I dried off, I put on the clothes that Alex gave me. A pair of shorts that were a little too loose in the legs and an old t-shirt that was way too thin.

Nice.

Still, clean clothes were better than dirty clothes.

I wiped the condensation off of the mirror. As I stared at my reflection, all of the immortal features stood out to me. Was this noticeable to everyone or just to me?

Right after the change, my mom told me that I looked refreshed. I told her that I had gone to a spa. She seemed satisfied with the answer and never said anything else.

I was still trying to discover all of the new things about myself. There was a theory floating around in my head that I should be able to read people and other things on a deeper level, like feeling emotions and intentions. That skill would come in handy in my current situation, but no luck so far.

I let out a sigh as I turned and reached for the door handle. Alex was waiting for me just down the hallway.

"Feel better?"

"As good as a captive can I suppose."

"You've always had a good sense of humor." He chuckled. "Thanks for not trying to escape."

"A deal is a deal." I shrugged.

As we made our way back to the kitchen, he stopped short in the living room. I stood there for a moment wondering what was about to happen and my heart began to flutter.

"Look, Amy. I'm sorry we are in this situation. I don't want to keep you tied up in the kitchen. You don't deserve it. But my boss is a dangerous man. If you see um, you will understand. Just cooperate a little longer. Please."

I nodded. What was the point in fighting right now? It would accomplish nothing. The antidote was done, and Xavier would be saving me tomorrow. Hopefully.

I sat down I the chair ad didn't put up a fight when he began to retie my hands.

"Good night, Amy." He said as he headed out of the kitchen.

"Good night, Alex."

He left the room without another word, leaving me in silence. I wasn't ready to go to sleep, but there was nothing else for me to do. It would just make it seem like there was less time between now and my reunion with Xavier. That was definitely a good thing.

My mind glazed over the events of the last few days as I drifted off to sleep. Some days, life was just exhausting.

A loud boom jolted me from my sleep.

"Did you let her take a fucking shower, Alex?"

Whose voice was that? It was so familiar. I strained hard to listen. I knew that voice somehow.

"I didn't see any harm in it. She's still here isn't she? It's not like she escaped or anything. I have the situation under control."

"That's not the point, kid. I knew this was a bad idea. I knew she would be your weakness. If you ask me, the last thing you have is any type of control over the situation."

"It's not like that Martin."

Martin? That's why I knew the voice. How could this be? Had he been on the other side, playing Xavier this entire time? He was supposed to take me to Xavier tomorrow.

"Please. It was her then, it's her now. You

wanna know the funniest part of all? She doesn't want you. And if that wasn't bad enough, she's literally sleeping with your enemy! What? Do you think she's thinking about you while he is on top of her? She's always been too good for you, boy."

A door slammed and the whole house went quiet. My heart began to race so quickly. Was I alone? Was someone more dangerous than Alex in here with me? Who left?

I focused hard to control my breathing. I couldn't hear the sounds around me if my ears were filled with the sound of my pulse and my breath. There were so many thoughts in my head. What was going to happen to me tomorrow? Xavier didn't even know he was being set up. We were walking into a trap and there was nothing I could do about it.

I tried to get out of the chair. Alex had done an excellent job with his ropes. I tried to rock back and forth in an attempt to break the chair, but the legs must have been anchored to the ground. I was stuck. A sitting duck. I stopped moving and focused hard on listening to my surroundings. My pathetic attempt to get out of the chair wasn't quiet.

After a while, everything was still silent. I must've been alone. Once the comfort of that began to sink in, my eyelids began to get heavy. I slowly started drifting back to sleep. Hopefully that wouldn't prove to be foolish.

CHAPTER EIGHT

Suddenly, I was being shaken and jolted from my sleep once again.

"Run, Amy!" Alex urged in a hushed tone.

"What?" If the wild look that must have been in my eyes didn't show confusion, my question should.

"Get out while you can. I'm sorry for all of this." Alex cut my rope with one quick slash from his knife.

I didn't hesitate. I scrambled for the door and

didn't stop running once I started. Last time someone told me to run, things went sideways fast. This time better not end with a gunshot wound.

Memories of that awful night came flooding into me. It was hard to push it out. Each step I took felt more desperate than the last. Once again on the way to Xavier. My unexpected knight in shining armor.

My legs were burning so badly. My breath was severely strained. Shortness of breath would be an understatement. I wanted to stop, but I knew that I couldn't do that. If I didn't make it to Xavier before Martin realized I was missing, it could be catastrophic. He had to know the truth about Martin. Well, what truth I had. I was so confused about what was happening. All I knew was that he wasn't who I thought he was. And I had to get him away from my mom.

I ran for my life before and I could do it again. Luckily, the house I was at wasn't far from Xavier's house. After a few blocks, the landscape began to look familiar.

It felt like I was in a movie. The way I was running between houses and through back yards felt so seamless. I guess immortality had its perks. Good thing it was late. It didn't seem like anyone noticed. It was necessary. I had to avoid main roads.

As I flung myself at Xavier's front door and began to pound, I had to fight to not lose focus. It was hard to stay in the moment and not go back. Last time I showed up like this, I was half dead and covered in blood. I guess the odds were more in my favor this time at least.

I was surprised to see a gun tucked into Xavier's waistband when he opened the door. I didn't even know he owned a gun.

"Amy? How did you get here?"

"I ran. Look, we don't have a lot of time and I have so much to tell you."

I followed him inside, trying not to distract myself with thoughts of how sexy he was with a gun.

Down girl. Now is not the time.

"I'm gonna kill Alex for this."

"X…" I hesitated. "This is so fucked up." My breath hitched. This was harder than I expected it to be.

"Just tell me, Amy."

"It's Martin. He's the one pulling the strings. It's probably been him the entire time."

"How do you know? What happened?"

"Martin showed up. He was furious at Alex

because he let me take a shower. There was a little yelling and then a door slammed. I didn't hear anything else until Alex woke me up and told me to run."

"So, Alex helped you escape from Martin?"

"In a nutshell."

"Where was Martin when you left?"

"I'm not sure. That's why we don't have much time."

"That son of a bitch." Xavier slammed his fist down on the kitchen counter. I jumped."

"Sorry. I know you are on edge. Come here baby."

I walked over to him, and he took me into his arms. My adrenaline was so off the charts. When I got here that a hug hadn't dawned on me

"Did he hurt you?" he asked as he began to look me over.

"No. I'm ok. What are we gonna do, X?"

"I don't know yet but I'm gonna keep you safe?"

"What about my mom?"

"That's complicated. She isn't safe with Martin. Unfortunately, the timing of it all might just make her think that you are just being dramatic and trying to break them up."

"Ugh. You're right." I know my mom. It's gonna be hard to draw her away.

"We will figure something out."

"I need to tell you something else. I don't know if anything could come from it or not… Alex knows that I'm immortal."

His body was still.

"How?"

"We were arguing, and it just came out. I wanted him to know that you're not a monster."

"Amy, I don't care what Alex Cardwell thinks of me."

"I know that. For some reason, I do. You are so much more than anyone realizes. I want the world to know."

"I love you, Amy."

"I love you too, Xavier."

I snuggled back up to him and sighed. Why can't life just be simple?

"Are we safe to stay here tonight or do we need to leave?" I asked with my face buried in his chest.

"We can stay here. We are gonna do things a little differently, though."

"What do you mean?"

"Come with me. I'll show you."

He took my hand and led me to his spare bedroom. I must have had a skeptical look on his face because he stopped and chuckled when he looked at me.

"Just trust me."

"I do."

He closed the door behind us.

"Walk into the closet and go to the back."

He sounded crazy but I did as he said. There was a wooden wardrobe pressed up against the back wall.

"Are we taking a trip to Narnia?"

"Something like that." He winked at me and made sure the closet door was secure.

He walked past me heading toward the wardrobe. He felt along near the edge of it, moving his fingers over the ornate details. An audible click sounded and echoed throughout the closet.

Slowly, Xavier swung the wardrobe forward, revealing a hidden walkway. He turned on a flashlight and handed it to me.

"Don't worry, once we get to the end we won't need flashlights." We can't use a real light because it might illuminate the wardrobe. We are better hidden this way."

I trusted the process and continued walking down the dark hallway. After quite a few paces, I could see a faint light in the distance.

At the end, I turned a corner and saw what looked like a little hidden apartment.

"You saw everything that was hidden at Nectar. Does this surprise you?"

"I guess it shouldn't." I chuckled.

"This space is soundproof and perfectly concealed. There is a bedroom, bathroom, plenty of food, and Wi-Fi."

"I will definitely sleep soundly down here."

"Why don't you make yourself comfortable and I am going to grab a few things for us."

"Are you sure it's safe?"

"I'll be fine. Just need to grab a few essentials. Be back in a jiff."

He kissed me on the forehead before disappearing.

I walked to the bedroom and sat on the edge of the bed. While I was a bit worried for Xavier venturing out by himself, this was still the safest I had felt in days.

Beyond safety. I was exhausted. God only

knows how far I ran. I was still wearing Alex's t-shirt and shorts Even though I recently showered, I felt disgusting. I got off of the bed and looked for the shower.

It was nicer than I would've expected for a smaller space. I shed the clothes of the biggest jerk I have ever dated and got in. What a pig. He had me tied up for days and he used that as an opportunity to try to get inside of my head. I was ashamed to admit that it worked. Just a little.

I washed everything from my head to my toes. There were no spots left unscrubbed. I tried to scrub away every bit of the last few days. Once I was finished, I dried off and hustled to the bed. When I got in the shower, I didn't think about not having any clothes to change into. I quickly slid under the covers and rested my head on the pillow.

Xavier appeared in the doorway. The gun was tucked into his waistband again.

"I grabbed clothes, snacks, and a few essentials. Everything is locked up. The alarm is set, and everything seems quiet."

I wanted to carry a conversation, but I was tired, and my brain needed to be recharged. And right now, Xavier was looking pretty darn distracting.

"Do you even know how to shoot that thing?"

He looked at the gun and smiled.

"Baby, just because I'm a scientist doesn't mean that I'm a pussy."

Why did that just turn me on so much? This sleep deprived, panicked state just made me feel so feral. I thought about it for a moment. Him being weak was never something that crossed my mind. I would've previously considered him to be docile. Not that it was a terrible thing. I was perfectly happy with him. This new edge I was seeing was definitely something I could get used to.

"Oh yeah?"

"Oh yeah." He put the clothes in his hand down at the foot of the bed. "I don't miss. A fool will fire with emotion. A smart ma is patient, surgical, and waits for the shot."

He pulled the gun out and placed it on the bedside table. I turned off the lamp as he crawled in bed. The sun would be up soon, and we needed to get some sleep. Judging by Xavier's moves, though, sleep seemed unlikely.

CHAPTER NINE

The sound of music woke me up and Xavier turned his alarm off. There were no windows down here. It was for security, of course, but it was a little disorienting, nonetheless.

"Good morning, beautiful."

"Too early."

I didn't know what time it was, but it felt like I had only been asleep for about an hour.

"Never too early when you're immortal."

"Says you."

Xavier laughed and I sat up.

"Ordinarily I would suggest we sleep in, but there is too much to do today."

"You're right. It's good to see you so motivated. I know things have been difficult for you lately."

"Thinking I was going to lose you somehow put everything in perspective for me. I was weak before. I won't make that mistake again."

He leaned over and kissed the top of my head.

"I'll go make us some coffee."

"That sounds great." I said as I stretched and tried hard to resist the urge to lay back down.

I grabbed the clothes that were still at the foot of the bed and picked out an outfit. I was just finishing putting it on when Xavier walked back in with coffee.

"Not nice making me miss the show little lady. I brought you coffee and everything."

I laughed as he winked and handed me a mug.

"What's our plan?"

"First, I'm going to call Nectar. I'll ask Janelle to phone me if Martin shows up. I can trust her not to say anything to him."

"Is there really an antidote?"

The question caught him off guard. He recovered quickly, but I saw the subtle wince immediately.

"Do you think I would risk your life?"

"I think that you are very clever."

He smiled bigger than I had seen in quite a while.

"Kind of."

"You gotta do better than that, Xavier."

"There is an antidote… for one of the immortality prototypes. Meaning the antidote for the real strain would be easy to calculate based on the revisions made for the final product."

"Thaaaaat sounds right." I laughed and enjoyed that we could still find good moments amidst the chaos.

"I was thinking about trying to call your mom next. Feel her out a bit. There could be a chance that she hasn't heard from Martin yet."

"Okay. What do I say if she answers?"

"Ask her to meet you at Nectar."

"That seems risky, but I trust you."

The phone rang five times before her voicemail began playing.

"No answer."

"That's ok. We will try again later. Don't let it worry you It doesn't have to be something bad."

"Yeah. I just hate not knowing."

"I know. Martin is smart. There is a particularly good chance that he will ghost your mom for a little while. At least until he has more information, He might be operating on the assumption that you have already told her about him."

"What's next?" I needed to change the subject. Getting upset about my mom was not going to help us right now.

"Let's figure out our main objectives. We need your mom. Security at Nectar needs to be beefed up. We have to figure out what Martin and Alex's next moves might be."

"We know they want an antidote, but why? No one even knew that the serum had been finished or used. I don't get it."

"Leverage. Martin knows how close I was before we moved to Andra. He is smart. If he was a betting man, I promise you he would bet on the serum being finished. I could have balked when Alex demanded the antidote. I could have tried to lie about the serum being successful."

"Why didn't you?"

"You." He shrugged his shoulders. It wasn't a brag. His demeanor gave off more of a vibe that suggested it was more selfless with a hint of regret.

I didn't know what to say.

"What if I was wrong and they already knew that it was finished. What if they knew that I made you immortal? That was a lie that I could not risk. They would have hurt you. That is one thing that I will not allow."

"I hadn't thought of that."

"I've thought about it a lot. Martin thinks that if he has the anti-dote, he will have the power. That's what it's always been about. I was simply too foolish to see it for what it was."

"So, the only way that this thing can really end is…"

The alarm went off. I jumped and looked at Xavier.

"Someone with perfect timing must be at the door."

"What do you mean at the door?"

"If someone were trying to break in, we would be hearing a different alarm right now."

Xavier pulled out his phone. He stared at his screen as I tried to peer over his shoulder. It was the front door camera.

"Alex."

I felt the blood drain from my face. Why couldn't I shake this guy?

"Stay down here." Xavier's voice was firm as he started to walk away.

"I'm coming with you."

"Like hell, Amy. I'm not risking it."

"In case you forgot, I am immortal too. I am strong. I am fast. I am *not* some weak little girl that you need to protect."

Xavier whipped his head around and although I could tell that he had something to say, silence hung around us. He turned back around, and I followed closely behind him.

The weight of my words began to drag me down as I really started to ponder the implications. If I wasn't a weak little girl, how was Alex able to keep me tied up for days? I immediately knew that was the question hovering in Xavier's mind. It had been the elephant in the room, and I didn't even know it. I didn't even know what the answer actually was.

This was not the time for this. All it was going to do was cloud my judgement.

"Close everything behind you, please." Xavier said softly as we began making our way through the closet.

I said nothing but did as he asked.

"What do you want Alex?"

"Xavier. I'm sorry man. I can explain everything, just please let me in."

"Why the fuck would I let you in my house?"

"I get it dude. You can kill me if you want damnit, but please just let me in first. If you don't, I'm gonna die on your doorstep."

Xavier shot me a hesitant look before turning the lock.

"Don't make me regret this dude." He yelled before opening the door.

As the door swung open, Alex fell into the foyer. He was bruised and bloody.

I gasped when I saw the state that he was in. Xavier quickly shut the door and locked it.

"What happened to you?" Xavier asked Alex before bending over and checking him for weapons.

"Martin beat my ass."

"Why?"

"Because I let her go." Alex yelled, his voice full of anger and pain. "I thought he was going to kill me."

"Why didn't' he?" Xavier asked. There was no

hidden humor or sarcasm in his tone. It was a serious question.

"I don't know dude. After I while, I just laid there kind of playing dead. He said he would be right back and left the room mumbling something about this being the perfect time. I managed to make it out of there before he got back."

"And decided to come here for some reason. Why is that?"

"Because I don't want to be a part of this game anymore. And because I needed to make sure that she made it back to you. I didn't know if Martin got to her or not."

"Part of this game? YOU are the one that started this nonsense years ago. Not me. Just years of you making my life and work hell whenever you could."

"Not me, Xavier. Not my idea, at least. Martin recruited me. It's been him even before it was me."

"You have two options right now. One. You let me tie you up. I want the information you have, and I don't trust you at all. Two. I put you back outside and see if Martin finds you or not."

Alex reached his hands out in front of him, wrists together.

"Tie me up dude. I'll give you what you want."

CHAPTER TEN

"Start from the beginning." Xavier commanded Alex, who was still sitting in the foyer.

"I was a low-level hacker just doing small jobs for a little extra cash. I had a podcast talking about conspiracies and topics that force people to actually think for themselves. I had a vision of creating a movement where people didn't rely on the news and government to tell them what to think.

Martin emailed me one day and basically offered me a job. All I had to do was talk to my audience about some scientific things. Martin gave me the topics and I just had to mention your name each time. All I needed to know was that you were a bad guy.

A little while down the road, I wanted out. Martin was creepy and anytime I questioned something, he would get super angry. When I told him I was done with it, he threatened my family, so I kept going.

In the meantime, I met James. He started helping with the podcast. He was always talking about how much he hated his dad being a scientist. I tried to tell him it wasn't all bad, but he never wanted to hear it. When he met Martin, it all got so out of hand.

Once Thomas died, it went off the rails."

My bottom lip quivered. Alex looked at me for a moment. His bloody, swollen eyes must have been hard to see through.

"The immortality thing has been a constant since then. Martin is obsessed. He always acted like he wanted the research to stop. Based on what I've seen since the fire, I don't believe him. There is something bigger going on."

"What happened after you let me go?"

"Martin lost his mind. I knew a fight was coming, but it was more than I was prepared for.

When he saw that you were gone, he didn't even say a word. He walked right over to me and started punching. He is stronger than he looks."

"What are you hoping to gain here?" Xavier asked sternly.

"I don't even know dude. Protection I guess."

"Why would I waste my time?"

"I'm the only insider info that you have right now. That should be enough until I prove myself."

"If you cross me, I won't hesitate to kill you, Alex. Your life doesn't mean jack to me, and I am not what you think I am."

"Got it."

"I need to move you. You can't stay here bleeding in my foyer. I'm going to blindfold you first. I don't want you looking around and gathering intel. As far as I am concerned, you are still working with Martin. I will be treating you accordingly."

Alex nodded but said nothing.

"Baby. I'm going to go get a blindfold. Make sure he doesn't do anything. Shoot him if he tries." Xavier handed me his gun and swiftly left the room.

I just stood there, staring at the man who represented some of the best and worst moments of my life. Why was I still being haunted by him? No matter what I did, I couldn't get away.

"I'm glad you are alive, Amy." Alex said softly. I stood there, saying nothing.

When Xavier returned, he placed the blindfold over Alex's eyes and stood him up.

"We are taking him where we were when he showed up. Can you get the doors?"

I nodded and scurried past him. I did everything I could to make sure the walk was seamless. I didn't want Alex to be able to count his paces and figure out how to get around.

Once we were in our hidden apartment, Xavier began leading Alex to the kitchen. He winked at me as he hit a button on the small kitchen island. It slowly slid out of the way, revealing a small staircase.

"Watch your step." Xavier said before not so gracefully leading Alex downward. He didn't push him down the stairs, so I would call it a win. I followed behind them until we arrived at what I could only call a jail cell. It was inside what looked to be some sort of panic room.

He sat Alex down on the floor before going back into the other room. He came back with a bottle of water and a first aid kit. He shut the door to the room.

"You can take your blindfold off now."

Alex took it off and looked around, slowly

blinking his eyes. It took him a minute to get oriented.

"I'll leave it up to you whether he gets cleaned up or not. He's made your life hell. It's your call." Xavier whispered in my ear.

I nodded. I didn't know what I wanted to do. Part of me wanted to see Alex suffer. The other part of me wanted every possible answer that we could get.

I took the first aid kit from Xavier and handed the gun back to him. I used the water he brought to wet a rag in the kit and wipe some of the blood off of Alex's face. Some of the lacerations were deep. They needed stitches. I'd never given anyone stitches before, but I was pretty good at sewing.

"You need a few stitches. Otherwise, you are just gonna sit here in bleed. Do you want me to stitch you up?"

"Yeah. I don't wanna die."

I grabbed the needle and thread from the kit and began to sew Alex back together as best I could. He kept the wincing to a minimum which I appreciated. When I was finished, I spread on a layer of greasy, antibiotic ointment. Something called Mupirocin. It looked like something you would have to get with a prescription.

"All set. Do you think there is anything on your body that needs to be addressed?"

"No, he mostly got my face. It feels like he broke a few of my ribs, but there's nothing you can do for that."

I stood up and walked back over to Xavier.

"Until I know that I can trust you, you stay in here. I will make sure that you are fed and not forgotten. For now, you need to get some rest. We are going to need a lot of answers."

We started to walk to the door when Alex started to talk.

"Amy. I tried to save your mom. I sent her an anonymous message telling her to be at this address today at noon. It also said not to tell Martin. She could only tell her daughter. I hope she shows up."

My heart raced. Why would he do that? Was this all one big setup?

"Why?"

"I'm not a bad man. Not anymore. And it's the least I could do after how I interfered with her life last time."

I cringed. I knew what he was talking about. My dad. How dare he refer to his death so casually.

"You better not be messing with me. Xavier's not the only one that you should worry about."

I stormed out of the room. I heard Xavier closing doors behind me.

"He can't hear anything we say out here. The room is soundproof."

"Good. That makes things easier."

"Are you ok?"

"Not really. Do you think what he said about my mom is true?"

"I honestly have no idea. It's hard to tell what his game is. Somebody did beat him pretty badly. His story makes sense. On the other hand, Martin leaving him alive and risking him running his mouth seems unlikely. I just don't know."

"There is something Alex said that has been bothering me."

"What's that?"

"Martin mumbling something when he left about it being the perfect time for something." I hesitated, not wanting to say the quiet part out loud. "That would be the perfect time to make him immortal. Xavier, do you think he got his hands on the serum somehow?"

"I don't see how that could have happened, but you are right. I thought the same thing when he said it."

"What are we getting into?"

"Something bigger than we realize, it seems. I highly doubt Martin would be the mastermind of something like this. He is smart, but not so conniving. There has to be someone he is answering to."

"Like who?"

"I don't know, but we will find out. First, we need to see if your mom shows up. We have to be here in case Alex is being truthful."

"I hope he is."

CHAPTER ELEVEN

"What time is it?"

I don't know why I chose to sit outside. It was bright… probably dangerous…and there was no clock.

"Why don't you just try to call her one more time?"

"Just answer my question, Xavier."

"It's 12:30." He said after letting out a sigh.

He was worried about me breaking down. That's not what he should have been concerned with. Right now, I was so angry I felt like I might explode.

"He's not gonna screw with me again."

"Amy, wait."

I didn't though. I flung the front door open and began making a beeline for the basement. Alex's chances just ran out and I wanted to be the first to inform him.

I knew that Xavier was behind me. Not just because I heard doors closing either. He felt like he needed to protect me. Everyone was about to realize I didn't need to be looked after.

Alex sat up when he heard the door to his room rip open.

"Why did you lie to me?" My voice echoed off the walls.

My hands were clenched into fists. I held my arms tightly to my sides, but I wanted to swing.

"What are you talking about?"

"So many lies you don't know where to start huh. MY MOM!" I shouted. He knew exactly what I meant.

"I didn't lie about your mom." He tried to defend himself, but I could barely hear him.

My pulse reverberated in my ears. Then in my

eyes. It didn't take long for everything to turn a bit blurry... a bit red. It was over after that.

I swung my fist hard and immediately broke through the stitches over Alex's left eye. Blood immediately covered my fist and each swing that I took after that was slippery.

"Don't lose your chance for any other information that you might want to get." Xavier spoke softly, clearly trying hard not to come across as making a demand. Smart man. For a moment, I had forgotten that he was even in here.

I looked down at Alex. His face was bloody again. Xavier was right. I did want answers. Would I be able to trust those answers at this point? Everything could be a lie. A bogus response to throw us off of Martin's trail.

An alarm snapped me out of my thoughts.

"The door again?" I asked, peering over my shoulder at Xavier.

"We need to go."

I didn't ask any questions. I just followed him out of the room, leaving Alex a bloody mess on the floor. Xavier stopped me once we made it to the kitchen.

"Wash your hands. Quickly."

I did as he said, still silent. Part of me was still

surging with adrenaline from what just happened with Alex. Part of me was afraid to ask who was at the door.

I washed the blood off of my hands and dried my wet hands on my pants. Xavier looked me over so quickly I almost didn't notice. Judging by his face, I would say my hands were clean, but I was still a little bloody.

"You haven't asked what is going on." Xavier remarked as we continued to make our way to the main part of the house.

"I'm afraid to. My mind… my heart can't take much more disappointment."

"Your mom is here."

There was an instant lump in my throat. I was happy, but somehow worried and scared too. Did she know anything? Was she in danger? Would she accept what we were about to tell her?

I was all but running toward the door.

"Be careful, Amy. We don't know if Martin is nearby."

"Have your gun ready then."

I opened the door to surprised eyes.

"Amy? What is this? Did you send me that message?"

"No mom, it wasn't me. Come in. I'll explain everything."

"Okay, but I can't stay long. I am supposed to meet Martin for a late lunch. That's why I'm a bit late. I lost track of time getting ready."

I ushered mom into the foyer and closed the door behind her.

"Hello, Xavier. Your house is beautiful. Am I correct in assuming this is your house?"

"Thank you, Joan. Yes, it is."

"Why don't we go have a seat in the living room."

Xavier led us to our destination. I was nervous. My mom had to stay here. If she were to leave after hearing the news about Martin, I don't know what would happen.

"Sorry I missed your call this morning sweetie. I have been meaning to call you back all day. You know how scatterbrained I can be. I haven't heard from you in a few days. What have you been up to?"

I didn't know what to tell her. Where would I even start? The part where her new man is a traitor or that he had me kidnapped? Instead, I was just awkwardly silent.

"Just tell her the truth, Amy. She deserves it."

I don't know if it was because we were both

immortal or if we were just on the same wavelength. He knew where my brain was right now, and he knew what I needed to hear.

We all sat down in the living room. I was on the couch next to my mom. Xavier sat across from us in a recliner. I nodded at Xavier.

"I don't really know where to start mom."

It was already hard trying to hold myself together. The second she grabbed my hand, I broke. I had to power through it. I let the tears slowly pour from the outside corners of my eyes down my cheeks.

"I was kidnapped a few days ago. That's why you didn't hear from me. I managed to get away yesterday and I have been here with Xavier since then."

"Oh my God, honey." My mom grabbed me and held me close to her. She slowly rocked back and forth. "And I couldn't even answer your call this morning. I am so sorry. Are you ok? Were you hurt?"

"I'll be fine. Physically no, I was not hurt. Emotionally... I am just a wreck. I will tell you absolutely everything, but I need you to promise me that you will stay here with me. At least until tomorrow."

"I will call Martin and cancel my plans."

"Why don't you call him after I tell you about everything?"

My mom nodded. I couldn't help but wonder what was going through her mind right now. I didn't envy her. This was not a position I wanted to be in either. She had suffered enough.

"I know it sounds crazy, but Alex is alive. He was waiting inside of my house when I went to check on things. He drugged me and kidnapped me. When I came to, I was in a house I've never seen before."

Mom said nothing. She just stared at me in shock.

"He was nice enough while I was there. He let me shower at one point. I knew that he took me because of something he wanted from Xavier. His boss showed up one night and discovered that Alex had let me take that shower. He lost it. Alex woke me up that night, cut my ties, and told me to run. I ran all the way here."

"Oh sweetie. Xavier, why didn't you say anything to me about this?"

"Joan, I'm sorry. I thought I had the situation under control, and I didn't want to worry you."

"Did you tell Martin? Surely he wouldn't keep a

thing like this from me."

Xavier hesitated. He didn't know what to say. It wasn't his job to deliver this news. I spoke up before he could.

"Mom… Martin…"

"What Amy?"

The words stuck in my throat. Her eyes said so much. Worry… panic… she was defensive too. I took a deep breath.

"Martin knows about all of it mom, but Xavier didn't speak a word of it to him."

"What are you saying Amy?"

"Martin was the one calling the shots, mom. He has been lying to all of us."

"Amy, I don't know what to say about this. I love you, but this is all very outlandish."

"Where was Martin last night mom? Was he with you?"

"No, he had work to finish for Xavier. Some last-minute project that he was running behind on. He was at his office at Nectar."

"Martin hasn't been to his office in almost a week. I monitor everything there. When Amy told me, I checked the footage. I needed to be sure."

"Where were you being held?" She said nothing

to Xavier.

"A neighborhood somewhere close to here. I don't know exactly where. It was dark and I ran as fast as I could. I cut through neighborhoods in case I was being followed. Finally, I recognized where I was, and I ran here."

"Do you remember anything significant about the inside of the house? You said you were able to shower, so you got to look around a little bit I'm assuming."

Her line of questioning was confusing me. I knew she would have questions, but there were not what I was expecting. I took a moment to think about the house.

"It looks like it was starting to be remodeled. The cabinets were outdated, but there were new appliances and fresh paint. There were new faucets in the bathroom. The sink seemed very modern for the rest of the house. Why are you asking, mom?"

She sighed and looked down at her hands that were folded neatly in her lap. Her aura was defeated. It was so strong that I could feel it. It made me sad.

"Martin purchased a house close to here. He closed on it a few weeks ago. He said he was going to flip it and rent it out. I think that is probably where you were."

"I'm sorry mom. Will you please stay here for a while? At least until we know things are safe?"

"I will… but Amy? You better start being honest with me."

"I am being honest mom. What are you talking about?"

"Little girl, it doesn't take a savant to notice the change in you. Now you are being kidnapped. You either have something they want, or you are something they want. I have been through enough because of all of this. I deserve some honesty."

"We can agree to that." Xavier said with a slight grin. "But once you're on our team, you're stuck."

"Agreed."

CHAPTER TWELVE

With all of the excitement, I forgot that Alex was currently bleeding in his room.

"I guess I owe Alex an apology and some more stitches."

"Yeah, I suppose you are right. I forgot he was down there for a moment." Xavier chuckled.

"What are the two of you talking about?"

Xavier and I exchanged a look. We agreed to be honest with her, but this was a bit much.

"Alex is here. After he let me go, Martin beat him up pretty badly. He came here for help. So he says, at least. Anyway, I cleaned him up and gave him a few stitches.

As I was leaving the room, he told me that he had messaged you anonymously telling you to come here. When you didn't show up at noon, I thought it was because he lied to me."

"Oh Amy. Is that why there is blood on your shirt?"

I knew it. I knew there had to be blood on me somewhere.

"Yeah. Don't feel bad for him. He killed dad. He deserves worse than I've given him so far."

"You have a point."

Mom quietly followed Xavier and I through our maze of hidden habitation. I offered to let her sit on the couch and not have to see Alex, but she declined.

When we entered Alex's room, he was curled up in a ball on the floor.

"I'm sorry. I guess I should have waited a little longer. Let me fix your stitches."

Alex said nothing, just nodded and sat up. He couldn't stop staring at my mom. There was so much sorrow in his eyes. I would normally think he was playing a good game, but this seemed different. I could feel sadness somehow.

"If either of you has something to say to the other, it might be a good idea to seize the moment. We don't know how long either of us has together."

I wiped his face off and carefully pulled out old bits of suture remnants. Once it was clean, I began to put his wound back together again. Hopefully this would be the last time.

"Mrs. Brown… I know my words will never mend a thing for you, but if I could go back and change my actions I would. I am sorry for the sorrow that I brought to your life. Any death I receive will be better than I deserve."

"If you are really sorry for what you have done to me, my daughter, my family… well, then you will do everything you can to help us move on from this never-ending cycle of bullshit."

I couldn't help but smile a bit. She was absolutely right. We *were* stuck in a never-ending cycle of bullshit.

"Yes ma'am."

"Why did you do this for my mom, Alex? It doesn't make sense to me."

"I knew she would be Martin's next bargaining piece. I have caused her so much pain. This was a good chance to gain back some good. It wasn't a selfless move, though. I want Martin out of my life. I can't live like this anymore. So, any chance I get to sabotage him, I will do it."

"Thank you."

"Don't thank me. It will never be enough. I know that."

"No, it won't."

I put another glob of antibiotic ointment on his wounds and walked back over to join my mom and Xavier.

"We will be back soon with lunch and some bedding for you. While making you sleep tied to a chair would satisfy me immensely, I don't want you to use it as a weapon in the future. So, snuggling yourself on the floor it is. When we come back, we will be expecting some answers."

"I'll answer anything you ask." He answered Xavier and we made our exit.

We didn't go far. When we made it to the kitchen we sat down.

"There should be enough food down here to feed everybody." Xavier said as he began rooting around cabinets.

"What are we gonna ask him?" I asked, unable to even think about eating food. My nerves were way to out of control.

"Anything you want. I have a lot of questions about Martin and what he knows. I imagine you might have some questions about your father or brother."

I nodded, pondering what I wanted to know. And what I was willing to ask in front of Xavier.

He pulled out a pot and pan and got to work prepping our food.

"Thanks for the remark about sleeping in a chair."

"No thanks needed. He deserves worse that what he's getting from us."

"Right? My tailbone still hurts!" I laughed and Xavier started cooking.

I sat there thinking about everything Alex ever told me that could have been a lie. Maybe I wouldn't ask about any of it. Did it even matter now? It wasn't like we would be getting back together at any point.

"Lunch is served." Xavier announced quicker than I expected.

I looked up at the stove. Grilled cheese?

"*With* salami."

"Very gourmet." I tried to say I my best Italian

accent. It was a bust, but everyone got a laugh out of it.

"I don't expect any of us to have an appetite right now, but we all need to try to eat a bit. No one needs to get depleted."

He was right on all accounts. His lunch did smell good, though. There was even a little side of marinara sauce on my plate. He poured each of us a glass of Coke and sat down to eat with us.

I ate my food slowly, savoring the taste. It took very little to recharge me now that I was immortal. I still enjoyed the flavor adventure of a delicious meal, though.

Xavier finished his meal first and excused himself to the bathroom after putting his plate in the sink. Once we were alone, my mom finally broke her silence.

"Your history with Alex is making this extra difficult for you."

"Is it that obvious?"

"Probably not so much, but I'm your mom. I know how you think. I also know how hard it was on you when Alex left. Despite what the history regarding dad and James, I know your personal history is affecting you."

"I can't let it, though. I gotta find a way to just

cut it all out. Why couldn't he just say dead?"

"You will get through this. You have always been strong, Amy. Since you were a baby, it has amazed me how resilient you were."

"Thanks mom."

I put my empty plate on the table with hers and stretched out for a minute. I knew we had business to take care of, but letting my stomach and brain settle a bit was a necessity.

CHAPTER THIRTEEN

I sat up slowly, looking around the room. Why did I feel so disoriented?

"Hey there sleepy head." My mom was still on the couch next to me.

"Why did you let me fall asleep?"

"Because you needed it. Xavier agreed."

I stood up and stretched.

"I didn't mean to zonk out. We have work to do. You didn't talk to him yet, did you?"

"Of course not. We were waiting on you, babe."

Xavier walked over and kissed me on the top of the head. The dirty plates were no longer on the table. I glanced into the kitchen to find all of the dishes clean and a plate with a sandwich sitting on the counter.

"I'm ready when you are. Is this for him?"

"It is. Are you ready? You can get your bearings first."

"I'm good. Let's get this over with."

With that we made our way to Alex. I wasn't sure if mom was going to want to be there or not, but she was right by our side.

When we walked into his room, I handed him his sandwich and stepped back.

"Thank you." He said quietly.

"Xavier, why don't you start." I suggested still unsure of what I was brave enough to ask.

"Do you know where Martin is right now?"

"My guess would be his new house. He purchased it using a fake name."

"What does he know about the immortality serum?"

"He knows it's finished. Well, he's pretty sure it

is. I don't know why he wants the antidote. He hasn't told me what he's going to do with it."

"Does he know…"

"That Amy is immortal? No. I don't know how, though. I could tell there was something different right away. You are too, aren't you?"

"I was going to ask if Martin knew that Amy made it here after she got out."

"Oh. He never said either way, but I think he assumed that she made it to you."

"What does Martin want?"

"To dethrone you… and to watch you fall."

"Why?"

"I don't know."

"Bullshit! You must have some sort of idea. You have been his lap dog for years. You're not stupid, Alex. You know how valuable information is. We both know you have a brain full of secrets right now."

"I don't know man. It's something personal. He would never tell me."

"I see you are just here to waste my time. Maybe you will have more to talk about when you are hungry."

Xavier stormed out of the room. I wasn't done

here, but we needed to regroup. I motioned for mom to go ahead and leave the room. I was behind her but before I left, I turned and looked at Alex.

"Was any of it real?"

"It all was, Amy. I love you."

I wanted to cry. I wanted to tell him that he wasn't allowed to say that to me ever again. Instead, I turned back around and locked the door behind me.

"He's lying. He would have to be a complete fool to spend that much time with Martin and not have all of the information that I seek."

Xavier was slamming things around the kitchen. I think he was opening cabinet doors just to slam them shut.

"Do you think he is holding out for some sort of leverage or is he just Martin's puppet?"

"I don't know." Xavier sighed, eventually making his way to the living room. "There must be a way to find out, though."

"We could go through some of his podcasts. There might be some information in there that could help us."

"That's a good idea. I've never looked at it before. The content he produced was not my cup of tea. Not to mention, he wasn't very kind toward me.

It never seemed like there was much of a point to it. Until now, that is."

"Why don't we go upstairs where it is more comfortable."

"Yes. I could use some sunlight." Mom chimed in and we made our way back up to the main part of the house.

Once we made it back to the main part of the house, mom put her hand on my shoulder.

"Are you ok mom?"

"I'm fine, but I think we could use a few minutes alone to chat."

"Of course. Xavier, we will catch back up with you in a few minutes."

He nodded and I followed my mom into what had become her temporary bedroom. We sat down at the foot of the bed.

"Sweetie, we need to talk about what Alex said in there."

He didn't know anything. I didn't know what she was hinting at.

"What do you mean? He said he didn't know anything. I'm sure it is a lie… but I don't even know what to believe anymore."

"He called you immortal, Amy. Don't think my

ears or my mind missed that."

I didn't know what to say. I didn't want her to be so wrapped up in all of this. Just be honest.

"I don't know what to say mom."

"It's true, yes?"

"Yes ma'am. It is true."

"I knew something was going on with you. No spa has ever made me look so refreshed."

"I'm sorry I wasn't honest with you. As you can see, all it has done is complicate things for me. I didn't want you to be dragged into any of this. In the end, I guess it didn't matter because you are in the thick of it anyway."

"So, it's come full circle. Your father died because of it, and you will lie forever because of it."

I was quiet for a moment.

"I hadn't thought of it like that, but you are right. The funny thing is that I almost died for it too. I didn't want to tell you some of this, but you deserve to know." I hesitated. I didn't want to tell her what a monster her son really was.

"You can tell me the hard stuff, Amy. I need to know."

"The immortality serum only works if you are almost dead. Luckily, I made it to Xavier just in time. He saved my life that night. There was no saving me otherwise." My eyes became misty as I thought about it all again.

"What happened to you that night?"

I took a deep breath and tried to steady my hands that I just realized were shaking.

"James chased me through the woods. I was trying to get away and I jumped into the river. I was hoping the current would help carry me away to safety. He began firing his gun into the water before I had the chance to make it very far. One of the bullets struck me and by the time I made it down river, I had lost a lot of blood. Almost too much.

I ran to Xavier's house and almost collapsed on the front patio. He called a doctor, but there was nothing they could do. When all other options were out, he injected me with the serum."

My mom was silently crying. I hated having to shed any more light on what James had become. She was such a good mom. Growing up, all of my friends were jealous of me because of it. This was breaking my heart.

"I'm sorry mom. I never wanted to have to tell you that story."

"I know, baby. Your bother wasn't always evil. When he was little, he was so loving and thoughtful.

The friends he made in high school led him so astray. When your father tried to reel him back in, he just pushed back harder. I never thought he would hurt you. God if I had, I would have sent him away. I would have done something."

"It's ok mom. He won't hurt me again."

"James is dead, isn't he?" Mom asked so quietly I almost didn't hear her.

I had been dreading this day.

"Yes."

"I had a feeling. Call it a mother's intuition. How?"

"After Xavier saved me, we ventured out. Me senses seemed heightened, and I wanted to see what was different now. James must've been waiting for just that. We ran into him. He was going to kill Xavier… but I killed him first."

"Oh, Amy, no." My mother quietly sobbed. I felt crushed.

"I'm sorry mom."

"You have to reason to be sorry honey. I'm sorry you had to be in such a position. I can't imagine what these past months must have been for you."

"I'm holding on ok."

"Don't keep all of this in next time. You know I will always be there for you no matter what."

"I know."

"We can talk more about this later. Let's get back to work. I'm sure Xavier is anxious."

She gave me a hug as we stood up. For the first time in months, a wave of calm rushed over me.

CHAPTER FOURTEEN

We decided that the best plan of action was to split up the work. Each of us would watch a third of Alex's podcast episodes. Mom and Xavier decided to watch on their phones. I opted for a tablet.

I knew about his podcast. He talked about it, but not in great detail. I never watched an episode. Some might have thought that made me a bad girlfriend, but I never thought he wanted me to see it. He never told me what it was called, where to find it, anything about the episodes… nothing.

As I pulled up my first episode to critique, I

was surprised to see a younger, much more vibrant Alex on the screen. He seemed happy, wholesome, not yet jaded. My heart ached at the thought of the man that he became. What could have been for him if Martin hadn't entered his life?

My first episode to watch was about chemtrails versus contrails. Still a controversial topic, but he presented it in a very nonbiased way. He just offered facts and encouraged his viewers to make their own decisions. I chuckled to myself for a moment. My dad would've hated Alex when we were together. Old Alex, though… I think my dad would have appreciated his approach.

I started to notice a change around episode 30. He started the show by talking about stem cells and whether or not they were a safe way to try to cure disease. By the end, he was talking about cloning. He took it so far. At one point, he suggested that a prominent scientist was kidnapping people for cloning experiment.

I knew it wasn't true, but it was still a hard thing to hear. You could see in Alex's face that he was spewing nonsense. Those once vibrant eyes now seemed hollow… cold.

I was getting through my share of the videos pretty quickly. If it was a slow or unimportant part, I skipped ahead. I developed a pretty efficient system.

We were all glued to our screens, so I wasn't sure how Xavier and my mom were doing.

After a few more videos, I paused. As I rubbed my eyes and stretched a bit, I thought about everything I had just seen. In each video, Alex seemed to be a little farther gone. He also never mentioned Martin.

Toward the end, he talked a lot about being censored. He began referring to himself as controlled opposition. It started as a joke, but it seemed to become a way out. I think he wanted his followers to know the truth. He just didn't know how to do that safely.

I glanced at the dates of the videos. He was still making these when we were together. How did I miss all of this? Was I really so wrapped up in my own grief and mission for revenge that I didn't notice?

I stood up and put my tablet down on the table. I had to talk to Alex. Xavier looked up at me. I opened my mouth to tell him what I was doing, but no words came out. I turned and started talking toward the passage to Alex.

"She needs to do this on her own, sweetie." I heard my mom say to Xavier.

"Thanks mom." I whispered, knowing that no one could hear me.

She was right. I did need to be alone for this. If I wasn't, Alex probably wouldn't be fully honest with me. I probably wouldn't be comfortable enough to ask the questions that I needed to either.

I walked slowly, closing the doors behind me. At first it seemed silly. Xavier and mom were still behind me. They could close them if they needed to. If there happened to be an attack, though, preparation now could keep me safe. The extra time it took would give me a little longer to go over my questions anyway.

When I finally made it to the door of Alex's room, I hesitated. My hand hovered over the doorknob. I wanted to turn it, but I was scared. What if I didn't like the answers that I was about to receive? Even worse… what if I did?

Alex was already sitting up when I opened the door.

"Are you alone?"

I nodded at him. Hopefully this wasn't a mistake.

"Go ahead. Ask whatever you want. That is why you are down here isn't it?"

"It is. Please Alex, I need you to be honest with me. Even if the truth is uncomfortable."

"I promise."

"I don't really know where to start." I laughed nervously. "I watched your podcast. The dates that you made them… we were together then. How didn't I notice?"

"Notice what?"

"How empty you were. It's all I can see in those videos, but I never saw it then. Why not?"

"It's complicated."

"Try me."

"Damnit Amy, we don't have to do this."

"Yes, we do. Just tell me."

I was on the verge of tears. I knew I would never have the courage or maybe even the chance to have this conversation again. I couldn't let this moment get away from me.

"It was both of us. You were very preoccupied. I did a decent job hiding how stressed I was when I was around you. It wasn't just because of Martin, either. I fell in love with you so quickly. The guilt of knowing the role I played in your father's demise weighed on me every day.

When you told me that you were going to work for Xavier, I felt such panic. The more digging you did, the closer you were going to get to the truth. It was just a matter of time before I lost you. That's why I left. The longer it took to cut ties, the harder it would be.

Looking back on it, I know I was a fool. Part of me hoped that if I just loved you enough, we could get through it if the truth came out. That could never have happened. I lost you before I even had you."

"Thank you for being honest. For what it's worth, I'm sorry I didn't notice."

Alex shrugged. He didn't have to say anything. I saw the lump he swallowed. He might be a monster, but he wasn't unfeeling yet.

"You need to be honest with Xavier. Please don't taunt him. The easier you make this, the faster we can all move on with our lives."

"I know that. It's just hard to be on his side for anything. Do I actually think that he is a bad guy? No, I don't. However, I spent a lot of years saying otherwise. Things are complicated."

"I get it." I looked toward the door. "We will be back later. Please think about how you will handle the questions. This is important."

I didn't wait for him to respond before I headed out the door. My pulse was racing, and I was eager to be out of the room with Alex.

Once his door was locked behind me, I took a deep breath. I walked to the bathroom and turned on the sink. I splashed a bit of cold water onto my face and stared at myself in the mirror. There were shadows under my eyes. My skin was pale. I definitely did not look good. Considering the rate that my body was supposed to be regenerating at, my appearance was a bit concerning.

I turned the sink off and headed back upstairs. Xavier would be expecting an explanation.

CHAPTER FIFTEEN

When I finally convinced Xavier to go back downstairs and give talking to Alex another shot, it was late. We were all on edge. Unfortunately, we couldn't move forward until this was behind us.

I knew that Xavier was not going to like reasoning for why I had to talk to Alex on my own. He claimed to be only concerned for my safety, but I didn't believe him. At least part of him worried that Alex and I still had interest in each other.

I don't know what hurt worse; the fact that he

thought I could be hung up on someone who killed my dad and kidnapped me *or* the fact that there might be some truth to it. I pushed the thought farther and farther down until it was no longer so prevalent.

My mom decided to stay behind while we questioned Alex. She was tired too. She would never say anything, but she didn't need to. You could see it. I felt bad about it. She really had suffered so much. She didn't deserve this.

"This is his last chance." Xavier turned and said to be when we made it to the door. "If he has nothing to give me, he can sit down here and starve."

"Agreed." I said as definitively as I could. I didn't know if it was a lie or not. Hopefully I wouldn't have to find out.

Alex looked just like I left him. A sad shell of a man.

"Last chance. I'm ready for some answers."

"Ok." Alex said quietly.

"Why?"

"Like I said before dude, I don't know. It seems like it is something personal. He didn't talk about it. All I ever managed to pick up on was a name. I don't know who the name belongs to or why it is important."

"What name?"

"Maggie."

The mood shifted instantly. Things felt painful.

"And you know nothing other than a name?"

"Not *nothing*. I did some digging. From what I can tell, I think Maggie might have been Martin's daughter. It also looks like she died shortly after she graduated from high school. It sounded brutal. She had been experimented on."

"Thank you. We will bring you dinner soon."

Xavier turned and left the room.

"Is that really everything you know?" I asked, hoping if Alex was holding back, he would trust me.

"That's everything."

I nodded as I left the room.

Xavier hadn't made it far. He was sitting quietly on the couch.

"What's going on?" I asked as I sat down across from him. Something had shaken him. Maggie was someone he knew. That I was sure of.

"This whole situation… the reasoning behind it… it's just not something I would have seen coming. I don't even know what to do right now."

"Who was Maggie to you? I felt your energy

change. There is no need to lie."

Xavier sighed, shaking his head as he chuckled to himself for a moment.

"I went to high school with Maggie. A few weeks after we graduated, she was found dead. She had been bludgeoned."

"Why would Martin be holding it against *you*?"

"The police questioned me about it because she was found close to a hunting cabin that I was staying in. I had an alibi, though. I was never bothered with it again."

"So, you have known Martin since then?"

"No, actually. I didn't know that he was Maggie's father. I only knew her mom. She always told me that her dad worked internationally. Her parents were divorced, and he was never around."

"So, the two of you were friends?"

"It's complicated. Maggie was an exceedingly popular girl. No one knew that we were friends. She was very clear that the relationship had to stay a secret.

We had a good setup. I did all of her homework and made sure that she got good grades and in return, she let me experiment on her a little. Nothing drastic or dangerous, of course."

I didn't know what to say. I just sat and quietly

listened to his story, scared of where it might be going.

"The night that she died seemed so insignificant until it wasn't. We spent the evening together. After I finished her calculus homework, it was my turn to get something from her."

He laughed a little.

"You have to understand, I was stuck between having a huge crush on this girl and thinking that she was a shallow brat. This is humiliating." He paused and rubbed his temples. With another nervous laugh, he continued.

"I thought I came up with a great idea to test how pheromones could affect someone. It was going ok until she asked what the experiment was.

It was going to be a multiple part experiment. Phase one involved applying them topically to my pressure points. During phase two, they were to be injected. Phase three was still in the planning stages.

The night that Maggie died was phase one. I applied the pheromones before I got to her house. By the time I was done with her homework, I thought they would have kicked in. She asked if I was going to start the experiment and I told her that I already had.

I was so awkward. I thought that wearing the

pheromones would be enough. That clearly wasn't working, so I decided to step it up a notch. I tried to make a move on Maggie. She didn't appreciate it and the pheromone experiment was a bust.

We had some pretty harsh words and I left. I went to the hunting cabin because I knew I'd be alone there. I was embarrassed about what happened. School days were behind me, but she was still going to tell everyone. The hunting cabin was a good place to think. I was going there to figure out how to handle the situation I was in.

What happened after that is anyone's guess. I don't know why Maggie was so close to my cabin. Perhaps she had more of a heart than I thought, and she was on her way to apologize. It could just be happenstance. Either way, I never figured it out."

Xavier stared off into the distance. His eyes were glassy. This was significant for him. Perhaps more so than he was letting on.

"What was her official cause of death?" I asked, trying to gather as much information as I could before forming an opinion.

"Blunt force trauma."

I shivered.

"So, what then? Does Martin think you killed his daughter? Why would he?"

"I don't know. I was only questioned because of my location. I don't even think they knew that Maggie and I were classmates. No one ever saw us together. Her mom was never there. She was dating some rich guy from Chicago and forgot that she had a kid most of the time. I was nothing to Maggie. He shouldn't have even known about me."

"We will get to the bottom of it. Let's get Alex some food and then go to bed. We need to rest."

"Yeah, you're right."

CHAPTER SIXTEEN

I woke up in a panic just after sunrise. It was something I was starting to get used to, unfortunately. This had been my routine for a while now and not just since I had been kidnapped.

Being immortal had proved to be incredibly stressful. It seemed like every day I was either fighting for my life or preparing for some kind of attack. I was ready for peace.

Xavier rolled over and put his arm around me. He slowly started rubbing my back. He never said anything, but I thought that he could feel my energy. Since I had become immortal, I could. It was like everyone, even animals, put off a frequency. Perhaps it was because my senses had all become heightened that I was able to notice this now.

"You ok?" he asked quietly as he continued to make small circles on my lower back.

"Yeah. Just a little stressed about everything. We still have a lot to figure out."

"We do, but none of it is worth what you are going through. I can *feel* you struggling. This might feel like a crapshoot right now, but we will be the winners at the end of this. Don't forget that, Amy."

"I believe you."

"Why don't I go brew a pot of coffee and cook us all a little breakfast. Meet me out there when you're ready to start the day."

"Deal." I nodded and he kissed me on the forehead.

I stretched as he left the room. He was right. This wasn't a battle that I was willing to lose.

I quickly showered and applied a little makeup. It was a silly thing, but putting on a bit of makeup always made me feel a bit better when I was feeling down. It wouldn't hurt to try it now.

"You look nice today, honey." My mom

complimented me as I walked into the living room.

"Thanks. It smells good in here. Have you eaten yet?" The fragrance of bacon and cinnamon filled the air.

"Nope. I think he is almost done with breakfast."

"How did you sleep?"

"Pretty good. Do you even need to sleep?"

I chuckled pretty hard. Before I could answer Xavier was walking in with a cup of coffee.

"Yes, we still sleep. Our bodies need to rest and regenerate too. We just don't require as much of it as you."

"Are you ladies ready for breakfast?"

Mom and I both nodded excitedly.

"I will bring it in here to you. Then we can sit and discuss our plans for the day."

"He seems chipper today." Mom said as Xavier left the room.

"I think he is just overcompensating."

"For what?"

"Me. He knows that I'm stressed."

"He's a smart man."

"That he is." I smiled as I smelled the food

getting closer. "And a good cook."

"Breakfast is served."

Xavier put three plates on the coffee table and sat down. We each gabbed one and quite began eating.

"So." Xavier started while still trying to swallow his bite of food. "I had an idea."

"Great because I had no idea where to even start." I really was relieved.

"There are so many moving pieces. I figured that we need to find a starting place and take this one piece at a time. So, Alex is probably the best place to start. He is here. Can he be trusted? I don't know. Probably not. I'll give him a chance to earn the trust, though."

"How so?"

"Let's revive his podcast. Alex 2.0 or whatever lame name he wants to give it. There will be conditions of course. He will not be allowed to leave here. He will have to tell the truth."

"That's not a bad idea. We just have to be sure to monitor what he says closely. He could use this opportunity to sabotage us."

"Do you think that he will? What does your gut tell you?"

"No, I don't think he will. It feels like he is

done playing games."

"Then it's worth a shot. Let's grab the asshole some breakfast and see what he says."

This idea gave me butterflies in my stomach. I hadn't given too much thought to what was to come of Alex. Shifting him to a position to be more present irked me. How could I ever move on if he was around? It was impossible.

I put on a brave face though and when Xavier returned with a plate of food, I followed him to Alex. Voicing any objection or concern that I had would just look bad.

This whole situation had to be awkward for Xavier. It would be awkward for me if his ex was locked up downstairs instead of mine. The last thing I wanted was for it to look like I still had feelings for him.

"Rise and shine. Breakfast is served." Xavier said before almost dropping Alex's plate in his lap.

"Thank you." Alex said meagerly.

"I have a proposition for you. It seems unrealistic to keep you as a prisoner here forever. We need to change our arrangement a bit.

So on that note, I have a proposal. You restart your podcast. I will supply you with whatever equipment that you need. Your content needs to be truthful, and you have to try to undo some of what you have done over the years."

"I can do that."

"You will have to continue to stay here, of course. I'm sure you understand why we cannot let you go at this time."

"Yeah, I get it."

"You say you are done playing on Martin's team. This is your chance to prove it. Help us turn all of this around and we will discuss what our next steps together are."

"I'm good with that. Do I have to stay locked up in the dungeon or am I going to get a little walking around room?"

"No, I guess not. You aren't getting free reign or anything, but I can make your stay a bit more comfortable. Keep in mind though, you should be walking on eggshells. By the end of the day, you will be a little more comfortable."

"Got it." Alex said before shoveling in the breakfast Xavier cooked.

I avoided eye contact throughout the conversation. I wasn't sure what kind of arrangement Xavier had in mind, but hopefully his plan kept Alex far away from me.

CHAPTER SEVENTEEN

"What are your plans for him? Where will he be during the day?" I asked Xavier as I tried to mentally prepare for adding Alex into our mix.

"It will require a small amount of remodeling, but I was thinking of just making the lower level his space. I would need to be sure that he couldn't get to the connecting passage. The door will have to change."

I wasn't expecting that. It would mean that our hiding spot would be compromised.

"You aren't concerned about losing the only safety we have?"

"We will still have it here. His presence won't change that. He won't know what is beyond the door leading out."

I nodded. He had a point. This was an inconvenient situation to navigate. I felt like I was constantly worried about either overeating or even worse, underreacting. I had been trying to play it cool, but having an ex locked up in your house would be awkward for anyone.

"What is really bothering you?"

"Everything really." I knew he could feel it. There was no reason to deny it. "Having him in my space sucks. I hate that he is here. It makes it hard not to think about my dad and impossible for me to move on. I'm just ready for this to be over."

"I know you are love. Just remember that this is all temporary. We don't talk about it much, but I know you can feel things too. It's our frequency. We must be more tapped into something now that we are immortal. I haven't quite figured it out yet."

"I'm just ready for a less stressful chapter."

"Me too. It's on the horizon. I promise."

"I'm gonna hold you to that."

"You better."

"So, where do we get a super-duper extra safe nothing getting through it type of door? I don't remember seeing them at the local hardware store."

"I have a guy for that. Let me give him a call."

He winked at me and for a moment, I thought that he was telling a joke. Then he pulled out his cell phone. Turns out he really did have a guy. Xavier was always full of surprises.

"*Hey Mike. How've ya been, buddy?*" Xavier started to speak to whoever answered the phone. "*Good to hear it. Well, you know how science life can be. Look, I need another door like you installed in the panic room. As soon as you possibly could. I'm on a bit of a time crunch. That's great, man. See you then.*"

I stared at him patiently as he hung up the phone.

"We will have a new door this evening."

"That's fast."

"Yeah, Mike is a good guy. In the meantime, do you want to go pick up some equipment for Alex with me?"

"You think it's safe to be out in stores like that?"

"Martin isn't stupid. He would never try anything in public like that."

"What about mom?"

"Let's ask her to stay downstairs until we get back."

Of course, mom agreed. I think she felt safer down there anyway.

It would probably seem silly to some, but I was a little giddy about getting out of the house with Xavier. It's something that we hadn't gotten to do much of. I always welcomed the opportunity to feel a bit more normal.

I convinced Xavier to stop for coffee and a snack on our way to the store. It didn't take me long to suck down my favorite drink, a white chocolate mocha latte. I used to grab one at least once a week, if not more. This was the first one that I had in months.

I savored every last drop. Xavier took his time sipping on his boring cold brew.

"You're awfully giddy." Xavier said with a grin.

"I haven't had a cup of my favorite coffee in a while. That hit the spot."

"It's good to see you smile."

"It feels good to smile. I miss it."

We pulled into the parking lot of the first of four stores we would eventually go to. It took the rest of the afternoon, but we managed to get everything we needed to piece together a pretty great studio. Alex had better appreciate it because he certainly didn't deserve it.

There was a large black truck parked in the street near the house when we got home. I hated how anxious it made me. Always on alert.

"Don't worry. It's just Mike. He's a little early."

Xavier waved toward the truck as he stepped out of the car. As if on cue, the driver door opened and a middle-aged man with sandy blonde hair and a hipster mustache got out.

"Sorry I'm a bit early." Mike said with a surprising southern accent.

"No worries my friend. We have a few things to bring inside and after that we will be free to help you however we can."

Mike nodded and headed back toward his truck. Xavier and I hauled all of Alex's new equipment into the house.

"Let's just drop it here for right now." Xavier said when we made it into the foyer. "We can haul it downstairs once Mike is squared away."

It took two trips, but we got everything inside pretty quickly. Mike said he didn't need any help, so while he gathered his supplies, Xavier and I brought all of the equipment downstairs. Mom was eagerly waiting on the couch when we walked in.

She busied herself with unboxing while we made a second pass for the rest of the boxes. It was nice having her with me. I hated the circumstances and I felt responsible for all of it. She was a good mom, though. She was always in my corner no matter what.

Once she was done unboxing, she popped into the kitchen.

"How about some lunch?"

"That sounds great, mom. I'm starving."

"Shall I make some for Alex?"

"Yeah, I suppose."

"And what about the Mr. Mustache with the nice accent?"

I laughed out loud.

"I don't know. Why don't you ask him? His name is Mike."

"Well, I just might. I always have fancied a man with a southern drawl."

"I think calling it a southern drawl is definitely an understatement."

Mom laughed as she made her way to the door to introduce herself to Mike and ask if he wanted lunch. I couldn't hear their conversation, but she was blushing as she walked back to the kitchen. She grabbed an extra plate out of the cabinet and started cooking.

Xavier winked at me when I looked his way. He didn't have to say anything. I knew he felt it. While I was happy that my mom wasn't letting the situation with Martin keep her down, I was still weirded out by the thought of her dating. It was going to take some time.

CHAPTER EIGHTEEN

By the time Mike finished installing the new door, it was time to eat. He joined us in the kitchen just as mom was serving plates.

"I appreciate the hot meal, ma'am." Mike said right before taking his first bite.

The sound that followed was a good indication that he approved of the food. It was no surprise. My mom was a great cook.

"It's no problem at all. I enjoy having people to cook for."

"What's with the extra plate?"

Mike motioned to Alex's plate with his hand holding the fork.

Mom and I looked nervously at each other for a second before Xavier spoke up.

"It's for the dog." Xavier said dryly, still eating his food.

"Ah. I didn't know you had a dog."

"Neither did I." I almost missed the grin on Xavier's face. If I had blinked, I wouldn't have seen it.

Mike was quiet for a moment before letting out a laugh.

"I tell ya what. I miss hangin' out with you Xavier."

"Yeah. It's been too long old friend."

"Well, I hate to eat and run, but I have one job left for today and I need to get to it. Besides, I'm sure your prisoner would enjoy this lunch warm better than he would cold. Although, something tells me that this little lady's food would taste good no matter how it's served."

"I second that." Xavier complimented.

My mom just waved her hand at both of them.

"Miss Joan, I do hope I will have the pleasure

of seeing you again."

"I hope so too, Mike."

She was blushing again. Xavier got up and walked Mike out. Mom and I got up and cleaned the kitchen until he was back.

"Joan, you sure made an impression on Mike." Xavier announced as he walked back into the room.

"He's a little young for me." Mom laughed a laugh that I didn't hear very often. It was nice.

"You ready to lock this place down and had it over?" I asked Xavier. I was anxious to get this over with.

"Ready as I'll ever be I suppose."

Xavier walked to the door and sighed. I knew this wasn't his favorite idea either. There just weren't a lot of options. He opened the door slowly.

"Come on out." Xavier called out to Alex.

After a moment, he appeared at the door. His bruises were all in various stages of the healing process. He still looked awful, though. The stitches probably needed to come out today.

"Your lunch is sitting on the kitchen counter. Eat. Then we can talk."

Alex nodded and quietly made his way to the kitchen. He didn't say a word as he ate the food on his plate.

I watched him carefully. Each bite he took began to anger me. I sat on the sofa, seething at the thoughts running through my head. My father, Andra on fire, being kidnapped, gaslighted… this pathetic man didn't deserve the mercy that he was being shown.

"Easy love." Xavier said quietly, snapping me out of the angry daze I was in.

"Sorry… and thanks." I took a slow, deep breath through my nose and exhaled through my mouth. I was stronger than this.

Alex fork clanged against his plate as he put it down and I jumped in my seat.

"Thank you for the food."

"I said you wouldn't go hungry. Whether you like to believe it or not, I am a man of my word." Xavier stood and closed the distance between the two of them.

"It's more than I deserve."

"Yes it is but nonetheless, this is where we are now. As you can see, we have gotten the necessary equipment for you to restart your podcast."

Alex looked around at the equipment and nodded.

"We will help you set everything up, but first

we need to go over some ground rules. To make it easy, I made a list so you don't forget them."

Xavier handed a piece of paper to Alex, instructing him to read the rules and hand them on the fridge. I glanced at the paper once it was hung. His handwriting was terrible, but he got his point across.

Number One: Never attempt to leave the area.

Number Two: Make no attempt to disclose location.

Number Three: Do everything possible to repair the damage.

Number Four: Stay away from Amy.

"It's a pretty simple list. Any questions?"

"No, I don't suppose so."

"Alright then, let's get the stuff put together."

We all worked quietly together, assembling the new studio piece by piece. I was relieved when we finally finished.

"Should I wait to start anything on air until I look less beat up?"

"What do you think?" Xavier asked after pondering the question for a moment.

"I don't know. On one hand, looking beat up

could catch attention. I could tell people that's what happens when you spread lies. On the other hand, it could just make me look like a busted-up hostage who is being forced to spread the message I was putting out."

"Well, let's hope people don't think you are a captive being coerced. Maybe they will just be happy that their former favorite podcaster decided to stop being a piece of shit."

"Touche."

"Let's wait until you heal a bit more. In the meantime, I am sure there is a lot to do to get everything set up."

"Speaking of being busted, I need to take out your stitches." I interjected. I was ready to be done with all of this. The sooner I took care of the stitches, the sooner I could get out of here.

I pulled a small pair of scissors out of a kitchen drawer. Alex sat down at the counter and I quickly snipped the stitches.

"This isn't a hospital. They are cut, but you can pull them out. You should wash them as well. The bathroom is through there." I pointed toward the bedroom.

"There are towels in the bathroom and sheets on the bed. There should be some clothing that will fit you in the closet." Xavier piped up.

"Thank you."

"You should also know that this area is constructed to be indestructible. If you try to escape, you will find that you cannot. It is bulletproof, fireproof, bombproof."

"Don't worry dude. I'd be a fool to pull something. I'm safe here."

"Ok then. There are plenty of provisions in the kitchen for dinner, so we will see you tomorrow."

Xavier ushered mom and I out and he shut the door behind us. Once we were out, he locked up and we headed back upstairs.

"I'm glad that's over with." I blurted out as we were walking back upstairs.

"Yeah, me too." Xavier responded.

"What's next?"

"Unfortunately, I think it's time for us to return to Nectar."

CHAPTER NINETEEN

Before we went to bed last night, Xavier and I went over logistics for going back to work. We had been doing a lot behind the scenes, sure, but we had not been meticulously keeping up with appearances.

"What are we going to do about my mom while we are at work during the day?"

It was my biggest concern.

"I've given it some thought, and it appears that we have two options. She either needs to stay downstairs with Alex or she needs to come with us.

If she chooses the latter, it will be up to her if she just wants to hang out all day or we can give her a job."

"You think she should be the one to decide?"

"I don't think we have an option. If she doesn't get to decide for herself, she could grow to resent us no matter what we decide."

I sighed. He was right. I didn't want him to be, but he was.

"Ok. That's where we will start then." I conceded. "Hopefully she will be receptive."

I was nervous approaching my mom's room. It was still early and I didn't want to bombard her if she was still in bed. Hopefully she was up already. I knocked softly when we got to her door. It was still closed, but I could hear her tell us to come in.

"Good morning, kids." She smiled as I entered her room. She was dressed for the day but was lying in bed reading.

"Morning mama. How did you sleep?"

"Not too bad actually. This bed is more comfortable than my own. I know you didn't just come to see if I slept soundly or not. What's up, sweetie?"

"Xavier and I think it's time for us to return to Nectar. At some point our absence is going to cause too many questions."

"True. Plus, you don't know how Martin might try to exploit the absence."

"We were hoping that you might want to come with us when we go to Nectar each day. It's safe there." Xavier quietly chimed in from behind me.

"I would love to come to Nectar with the two of you. I don't want to feel like a charity case, though. Give me a job. I don't care what it is. Amy knows what I am good at."

"You are not a charity case. I promise. We just want you to be safe and comfortable." He smiled so genuinely.

"Thank you. I don't know what I would do without you kids."

We gave mom a kind of group hug. It was nice having her around. I appreciated how kind Xavier was to her. My mom was such a wonderful person. She had a laugh that could bring a smile to anyone's face. She could be a friend to anyone, but God help you if you crossed her. She was the best mom.

The last few years had been rough on her. I'd love to have the chance to make some of it up to her. She deserved it.

"We are planning to go back tomorrow if it works for you. We could leave here around seven."

"Sounds good to me."

Xavier and I walked back to our room. He grabbed a change of clothes as I snuggled back up in bed.

"What are you doing?" he asked with a smile.

"I do all of my best thinking in bed. You should join me, and we can have a brainstorming session."

"This seems counterproductive, but I'll give it a try."

"That's one of the things I love about you. Your sciency nature. You are always down for an experiment."

"Sciency?"

"Yep. Say what you want. You know it makes sense."

We both laughed as Xavier got into bed with me.

"Ok. We need to finish our game plan. We are returning to Nectar tomorrow, but why? What is our objective?"

"You weren't kidding, were you? Part of me thought that the brainstorming might be a fun ploy to get me into bed with you for… other purposes."

I laughed heartily.

"Sorry dude. I was being serious. Most of my good ideas start here."

"Ok. I'll give it a shot. I let myself be consumed with the immortality serum for so long. I lost sight of everything else."

"So where do you start? What's first?"

"I need to check on the clinical trials. That is our best chance for a breakthrough. There is some great research being done in here."

"That makes sense."

"What about you? What are you hoping to accomplish?"

"Well, the clinical trial thing would help me if there were good news. We need to keep getting our name out there for good reasons if we want people to forget what Alex and Martin fabricated."

"Ok. That's where we will start then."

"What job are you thinking for mom?"

"That's a terrific question. I was actually hoping that you would make that decision. You know what she's good at."

"Put the puppy dog eyes away. I'll do it."

"Thank you. I had no idea what to even suggest."

"Well, mom was a candy striper when she was a

girl. After that, she always worked with patients in some capacity. I think something in the clinical trial would be great. Any ideas?"

"Absolutely. I need someone to go around and speak to the patients each day. You know, sort of check in, see how they are doing, ask them a few questions."

"That would be convenient too since you are going to be focusing on the trials. We could keep her close without making her feel like a child."

Xavier stretched his arms out wide before rolling over and draping his arm over me. He kissed my forehead lightly.

"You were right. These bed brainstorming sessions might not be a bad idea after all."

"I told you!" I laughed. "And look how fast that was. We have most of the day left for whatever we want."

"So how do you want to spend out last day off?"

"To be honest, I'd love to go to the creek. I don't want to worry about Martin lurking somewhere the whole time though."

I missed the creek. Xavier and I used to go a lot right after the change. With our senses heightened, the experience was different. From the different paths and velocities of the current, to the varying temperatures through a single stream of water, there was a lot to take in.

It was a terrific way to train our brains to focus on many different things at once, while also having an enjoyable time with each other. As life got increasingly complicated, our trips dwindled.

"Fuck it. I'm done letting someone influence my life the way he is. Let's go to the creek."

I felt the smile erupt on my face. I could get used to this ballsy Xavier. I hoped that he was around to stay.

I bounced out of bed and grabbed my bikini out of the dresser drawer.

"Want me to invite your mom while you get ready?"

Yes, please!"

I knew that she would decline. She wasn't a very outdoorsy person to begin with. Even if it was something that was an interest for her, she would feel like an imposition.

Either way, I quickly got ready. I was eager for this alone time. I kept it simple with a bikini and a comfy summer dress. Flip flops finished off the outfit. No makeup. There was no point in it. I knew I would spend all of my time in the water.

"That didn't take long." Xavier said as he entered the room.

"What did mom say?"

"She declined. I made her promise me that she would be on high alert. If nothing else, she can lock herself downstairs with Alex."

I shot him a weird look but then nodded my head. He was right. If something went wrong, she could lock up with Alex. The chances were low that their spot would be found, let alone broken into.

"Well, I am ready when you are."

"I guess so." He said with a smile, slowly eyeballing my outfit.

"My eyes are up here." I laughed.

"I'll be ready in five minutes."

I grabbed a towel and my sunglasses and headed to the foyer.

"Have some fun today, sweetheart. You deserve it."

Mom spoke as I walked by her door. I stopped and turned around.

"Thanks, mom. If you need us, please call. Even if you are unsure. I'd rather be safe than sorry."

"I promise. Enjoy your day."

I smiled at mom as Xavier rounded the corner, almost bumping into me.

"See? Five minutes."

"Good job."

We locked the door behind us as we left the house. Xavier loaded a duffel bag into the car before he got in.

"What's in the bag?"

"Snacks and guns."

I laughed loudly.

"You're not kidding, are you?"

"Nope. You might be immortal, but you still get hangry. And guns are never a bad idea. Especially these days."

"You have a point."

Xavier laughed as he started the car and backed out of the driveway. I picked a station on the radio and relaxed in my seat.

It was nice to feel normal for a moment. I could tell Xavier felt the same. The frequency in the car was calm and harmonious.

I needed more trips like this in my life.

CHAPTER TWENTY

It was quiet at the creek when we arrived. There wasn't another car in sight. Other than an occasional kayaker, the place should be ours.

"Race you down to the water." Xavier gave me a wink before taking off.

We were faster now. I didn't quite understand all of it. To be honest, I didn't want to right now. There would be plenty of time for that later.

As I charged through the woods toward the sandy bank up ahead, I quickly flashed to that night with James. I shook it out of my head. I refused to be a victim.

Xavier barely beat me to the water.

"You got a head start." I yelled as I made it to him.

He laughed as he placed our things on the sand.

"But I was carrying all of this stuff."

The water was high today. That meant two things: there was not enough shore to lay out on and the water was deep enough to dive in.

I shimmied out of my shorts and tank top and backed up a few paces.

"Be careful." I heard Xavier say before I ran and took a nice, high, almost made me feel like a superhero jump into the air. I dove deep into the water, barely grazing the bottom.

When I popped up out of the water, Xavier was finally starting to get in.

"Took you long enough." I yelled out as he swam toward me.

He hit the surface with his hand, splashing water my way. I just giggled as I stretched out, floating on the surface. As I started up at the clouds above me, I heard Xavier sigh.

"I know we are supposed to be having a

relaxing day out, but I can't get everything off of my mind. I'm sorry." Xavier laid back and floated his way to me.

"You don't need to apologize. It's on my mind too. I wanted one day to forget everything and try to feel normal, but I don't even know if that is possible anymore. Seems like there is always something looming over us."

"I know what you mean. I can't tell you how many times my thoughts have drifted off to us living a life where we were just left alone."

"Left alone sounds nice." I sighed.

Silence hung between us for a few minutes as we floated slowly downstream.

"I need to ask you something, Amy."

I felt the awkwardness in the air before he even spoke up.

"You can ask me anything, Xavier. I'm an open book." It was the truth, although I was a little nervous about what he was going to ask.

"With Alex being around... both here and while you were being held captive... is it..." he trailed off.

"Are you wondering if there is some sort of unrequited love thing going on here?"

"Basically."

"I get why you ask. I probably would too. The answer is no. There is nothing there. Even if I was stupid enough to go down that rabbit hole, at the end of the day, he is responsible for my father's death. The fact that he is even alive now should prove that miracles can happen because trust me, I want his life to end. Right now, he is on borrowed time as far as I'm concerned."

"Got it."

"I love you, Xavier."

"I love you too, kitten."

The subtle ripples of the water were soothing. I could float all day.

"What's our next move babe?"

"I think I want to be interviewed on Alex's podcast. Might as well go for the gusto. I think it will make Martin make a move. If he doesn't, then we will."

"Do you know how his first two episodes turned out? I haven't had it in me to find out on my own."

"Pretty well it seems. Not as many viewers as before, but a lot more than I expected. I think there were enough viewers to justify making this move."

"And if Martin doesn't bite?"

"Then I'm going to tell him I want to talk

about Maggie.”

“That’s bound to get his attention.”

“I’d say so. I’m ready for this to be done. I want a normal life.”

“Me too.”

As we continued to float, we remained quiet. Our minds both seemed to be a bit more at ease. The sun was high in the sky but was making its way west.

“We should probably get going soon.” I said hesitantly, not wanting to leave. I knew that we needed to, though.

“Race you back to the start.”

I didn’t bother responding. I flipped over and took off. I swam quickly underwater. I was faster this way. Now that I was immortal, I could hold my breath for an exceptionally long time.

In no time, I swam past the spot where I grazed the bottom when I dove in. I came to a stop and poked my head out of the water. I was half expecting Xavier to have beat me, but he wasn’t there. I looked behind me, but he wasn’t back there either.

As my heart began to panic and my adrenaline spiked, I felt something by my legs.”

“Son of a bitch. You scared me.” I said, not

knowing if he could hear my underwater.

I felt his hands slip up, pulling at the sides of my bikini bottom. I squirmed away and he surfaced.

"Why'd you push me away?" He laughed as he wiped the hair off of his face.

"Because you never know when a person might come by."

"You worry too much. We haven't seen anyone out here all day."

I stuck my tongue out at him playfully and he surged my way. Before I knew it he had me in the air, flung over his shoulder.

"What are you doing?" I asked in between laughs.

"I'm doing this caveman style babe."

I laughed as he carried me to the car. I had to admit, I was kind of impressed when he managed to open the door, throw me in, and get in on his side before I had a chance to react.

"You eager to get home and be on the podcast?"

"No, I'm eager to get home and be on you." He winked at me as he threw the car in reverse and made his way back home.

"You don't have to wait until we get home." I

said quietly. Someone with normal hearing probably wouldn't have even heard it. With our heightened senses, I knew Xavier would hear me.

"Oh yeah?"

I nodded.

"Don't play with me girl."

"I'm not."

Without hesitation, Xavier pulled the car off on some side trail in the woods I never even noticed any of the times we came here in the past.

"Last chance." He said with excitement in his voice.

I blew him a kiss. I don't know why I decided to start playing this game, but I enjoyed it. The spice. The excitement.

By the time I heard his seatbelt unlatch, he was already on me.

I wasn't going to make this an easy game to win. I slid out from under him and got into the driver seat.

I laughed when he turned around and saw where I was.

He grabbed my ankles and pulled me down to him. In a flash, I was right where he wanted me all along.

REIGNITED

I lost.

CHAPTER TWENTY-ONE

When we made it home from the creek Xavier had two things on his mind: a shower and the podcast.

I thought about taking a shower after him and not joining him downstairs for his talk with Alex. I meant it when I told him that I wanted Alex dead. Not only had he killed my dad, but he got into my head after he kidnapped me. He made me question myself and how I felt about him.

He was a manipulative son of a bitch and he could not be trusted. Anything he had done up until this point was just to gain ground. Xavier shouldn't be alone with him.

I opted to hop into the shower with Xavier so I could be with him. I wanted to keep an eye on Alex. My dad used to always tell me to keep your friends close and your enemies closer. I aimed to start doing a better job of that.

After the shower, we both dressed quickly.

"Do you know what you want to talk about with Alex?"

"No, not really. I just feel like there is a good chance that this will make it to Martin. I don't want to play the final card in my hand. I'll figure it out when we get down there."

I gave Xavier a quick nod as I pulled a shirt over my head. Part of me was dreading the conversation that might ensue, but I still felt recharged from our swim. Thank God that came first.

"I'm ready when you are love." I said as I rubbed his back.

He headed toward and I followed behind him. I wasn't planning on saying anything. I was banking on being moral support… and maybe protection. Not that Xavier couldn't hold his own. I wasn't trying to be his knight in shining armor, but I wasn't a damsel in distress either.

Our walk was silent. I thought about making small talk, but I didn't. I'm sure Xavier was trying to mentally prepare for it all.

Alex looked surprised when we walked in.

"Hey guys. What's up?"

His friendly tone instantly annoyed me.

"We need to talk." Xavier said as I closed the door behind us.

Alex stopped what he was working on and gave Xavier his full attention.

"What do you ultimately want? Freedom?"

"Yes. And protection."

"That's going to be awfully hard considering Amy wants to watch you die. How about protection for Martin."

"I would accept that."

"Fine. My terms are simple. I want to be on your podcast. No bullshit. No spinning things in a way just to attempt to discredit me or make me look like a douche bag.

"Fine."

"Amy, does that work for you?" Xavier asked, catching me off guard.

"I can agree to that." I appreciated that he didn't try to offer Alex protection from me. That I couldn't agree to."

"Perfect. Alex, when can you be ready?"

"Well, I had an interview scheduled with a pretty important doctor spearheading the carnivore diet. I could try to postpone it."

"If you could please. I will be back in two hours."

Alex nodded.

I followed Xavier out of the door and breathed a sigh of relief once it was closed.

"That went pretty good."

"Yep." He replied, clearly having a mind full of thoughts.

Two hours passed by quickly. We didn't talk much. I expected to go over potential talking points and maybe have a few mock questions. Instead, Xavier stayed inside of his head. That's fine.

Truth be told, I would be happy when this part of the day was over. It was stressful. I've never really handled stress well, but with so much going on in my life lately, it is even worse. I took a deep breath and tried to clear my mind before we headed back down to Alex.

"Are you ready?" I asked Xavier once I heard his alarm chirp.

"As ready as I'll ever be."

He gave me a quick kiss on the head and we headed in Alex's direction.

"If he screws this up, I give you permission to kill him."

"Now you're making this hard. I want it to go well, but I also want him gone…" I winked at him and we both chuckled.

Of course he knew that I wanted it to go well. As much as I hated Alex, I loved Xavier more and wanted the best for him.

"Are you ready?" Xavier asked Alex as soon as the door was open.

"Sure am." Alex replied with a chipper tone. "I rescheduled the carnivore guy until tomorrow so we can do this for as long as you would like to."

"You remember the rules?"

"I do. Don't worry. I have to intentions of crossing you."

"Let's get to it, then."

I sat down on the couch to observe. Alex gave Xavier a pair of headphones and they sat down. Alex gave him some sort of countdown and then they were off.

Welcome back, friends. I have a special guest this evening and who it is might shock some of you. I know I have disagreed with him in the past, but we were able to talk recently and it has done a lot to clear the air. Everyone in the chat please welcome Xavier Holland of Nectar Corp.

Thank you for having me today, Alex.

I'll be honest with you doc, a lot of my followers probably thing you are an evil, greedy man. It comes with the territory. What do you have to say to that?

I can see how they might think that, but I assure you it is untrue. My science is a lot more boring than some might think.

What is the top thing that you are researching right now?

Well, we are running a couple of clinical trials that are proving to be quite promising.

May I ask what kind of trials? Are you allowed to disclose that?

The primary ones are for Parkinson's and COPD. The drugs for each are a totally novel approach. Something completely different than what is on the market now.

What makes them different?

To put it simply, they are safer options. There are fewer side effects and it is easier on the body.

And why is that?

It is because they are natural. It might shock a lot of people to find out that we aren't testing new, expensive therapeutics. If the trials are a success, people aren't going to find out that the treatments cost $1,000 per pill. What good is a cure if you can't afford it? Money shouldn't dictate life like that.

Wow. I promise you that no one was expecting to hear that. So, are you against big pharma or did you just want to take a different approach?

I have never been a fan of big pharma. Being young and in the profession that I am, people tend to make a lot of assumptions. Just because I am successful doesn't mean I am in some sort of elite class of dirty millionaires. I don't want any part of that.

Do you think that thought process represents your company as a whole, or is it just you that thinks that way? What about your second in command, Martin. Does he agree?

While I cannot speak to Martin's thoughts or beliefs, I can say that he is no longer with Nectar Corp.

That seems like a new development. Anything juicy there that the followers will want to know?

Nothing scandalous. Sometimes there just has to be a parting of the ways in life, but I wish him all the best.

The interview continued for about three hours. Xavier did such a fantastic job. Some of Alex's questions weren't easy, but it didn't slow him down. Before we left, Xavier extended his hand to Alex.

"You didn't take it easy on me, but you didn't pull any punches either. Thank you."

"We had a deal. I am a man of my word." He grasped Xavier's hand and gave it a shake. "Off the record, how many of your answers were bullshit?"

"None dude. I told you, I'm not the asshole psychopath that you think I am. If you get any bites from Martin, please let me know.

"Will do."

Xavier turned around and opened the door, letting me lead the way out of the room. Once it was closed behind us I left out a sigh of relief.

"What did you think, love?" Xavier asked as we walked to our room.

"I think you did a fantastic job. Coming from a PR gal, I hope that carries some weight."

"It does. Now we just wait to see if Martin takes the bait."

"And if he doesn't?"

"Then unfortunately, I will have to go with Plan B. And I really don't want to."

I could feel his vibe turn dark… cold. It made me shiver. I didn't know what Plan B was. He hadn't told me. I asked about it, but he said even talking about it made him feel bad. I decided to drop it after that.

CHAPTER TWENTY-TWO

It had been three days since the podcast and we hadn't heard a peep out of Martin. Even mom tried messaging them, asking to talk. He never replied. I didn't ask her to. I think she wanted to know if what they had was real at all or not. She deserved to know.

Xavier had been growing more anxious and was acting disconnected as a result. I understood. I would probably be acting the same way if I were in his position. Whatever he was planning seemed painful to him. It felt deep.

I was staying pretty silent. I didn't want to put any more pressure on Xavier than he already had. Alex swore he hadn't heard anything either. Xavier seemed to believe him.

I pushed my chair back from my desk and stretched. Part of me was glad to be back at work, but I also missed not having an agenda each day. It was almost noon. I had gotten into the habit of finding my way to the clinical trial floor to meet mom for lunch every day. Xavier was at my door when I opened it.

"Argh!" I yelped as I jumped a little.

"Didn't mean to scare you. I knew you'd be leaving to head over to your mom soon. I thought I would walk with you."

"It's ok. I just didn't expect to see someone at the door when I opened it. I'd love for you to walk me. What have you been up to today?"

"Not much. I haven't been able to get this thing with Martin out of my head to be honest with you."

"I'm sorry. Anything I can do to help?"

"Not really. I think we need to take the next step tonight, but I don't want to talk about here."

"I understand. You can tell me when we get home."

He kissed me on the head and led me out of the office. I put my hand in his as we walked to the clinical trial section.

Mom was excited to see that Xavier would be joining us for lunch today. I think he was just looking for distractions, but I was happy to have him either way.

"I ordered delivery for us. If you ladies want to join me in my office, I have it all set up."

I was excited to see a bag from Marciella's Italian Eatery sitting on his desk when we walked in. They made the absolute best lasagna. Their white sauce was like liquid gold.

"I love this place!" I beamed as I took a big, satisfying sniff of the air.

"I know. That's why I got it." He winked at me and I smiled back.

There was a little bit of everything. We each grabbed a plate and had a little variety sampler. Thank God I still needed to eat as an immortal. That alternative would have been tragic.

"I'm gonna want a nap after this." I laughed before eating another bite of shrimp scampi.

After we were all finished, Xavier packaged up the leftovers and stuck them in the refrigerator disguised as a filing cabinet.

"Well, I should be getting back." Mom said as she brushed crumbs off of her skirt.

"I'll walk you mom."

"No sweetie, I will be fine. You kids finish your lunch."

Neither of us protested and mom left the room. I stretched my legs out as far as I could and slouched in the chair. It was awkwardly quiet.

"How much longer do you want to work today?" I finally broke the silence.

"I don't have much more to do today. I'll probably be wrapped up in about two hours. Does that work for you?"

"Yep. That's great."

"Sorry if I have been off the past few days. I just didn't want it to come to this."

"I know you didn't. You have tried everything else there was to try."

"When we get home today, I will go over the plan with you. I don't want to do it here."

"I understand. Go get the rest of your work done and I will see you in a couple of hours."

He gave me a smile that almost seemed forced and left. I would be happy when all of this was behind us. Was I just destined for drama?

I walked back to my own office to busy myself for the next couple of hours. Since we came back to work I had been working on a piece that would be featured in a popular science journal. Xavier didn't know about it yet. I wanted to surprise him. He needed something like this to turn his career back around and move on from the dirt Alex threw his way.

My fingers felt like they were typing at a world record speed. When my phone chirped, I jumped. It was Xavier letting me know he was finishing up and would grab my mom on his way. I stretched my arms wide and closed my laptop. That was enough for today. I let Xavier know that I would grab our leftovers and meet him in the lobby.

I talked the entire way home. I probably annoyed mom and Xavier. I couldn't help it though. There was too much nervous energy to contain. I almost thought I heard someone sigh when we pulled up to the house.

Even though I was eager to know the details of Xavier's plan, I resisted the urge to approach him about it. It needed to be on his terms. Whatever it was clearly weighed on him heavily. We both headed silently to the bedroom to take off our shoes and get more comfortable.

"I know you are ready to hear everything. I'm

sorry if not knowing has been tough on you. You are a planner after all. I do appreciate that you have left me alone about it. You're a good woman to me."

"As bad as I have wanted to mentally prepare, I didn't want to add to your burden. You have enough on your plate."

"It's a simple plan, really. I'm going to send a text message to Martin. I do not expect him to take the bait at first." Xavier hesitated. "Then I will tell him that it is about Maggie."

I could feel his sadness, I didn't know what to say.

"The air must be cleared. He thinks I killed his daughter. I at least deserve a chance to explain what happened that night."

"And if he won't listen?"

"Don't you worry about that, kitten. I am innocent. There is nothing to fear."

"If only it were that easy."
"It can be. You just have to believe it to be so."

"After you get a response, what will you do?"

"Try to initiate a meeting. Explain things to him. Hopefully call a truce."

"And if not?"

"Then Martin will have to die. I refuse to live out our days looking over our shoulder."

Xavier pulled out his phone and looked at me.

"It's now or never I suppose."

I nodded and he began to type.

"I'd like for us to have a talk."

We sat and waited, not knowing how long or even if we should wait for a response. It took about five minutes for the phone to ding and when it did, we both jumped. Xavier almost dropped the phone.

"No thanks."

It was exactly what Xavier expected. Martin declined.

"About Maggie."

"You have some balls mentioning her Xavier."

"And you have it all wrong."

"I'll give you one chance. Meet me at Kylie Park tonight at ten."

"See you then."

CHAPTER TWENTY-THREE

I was a bundle of nerves. There was an infinite number of possibilities for tonight and my brain was obsessing over every one of them.

Mom agreed to stay locked up with Alex while we were gone… and to keep a gun on her. I didn't want to take any chances.

I concealed a gun everywhere I could fit one on myself. Who knew what Martin might have up his sleeve.

"You need to calm those nerves baby. I can feel

them all the way over here."

"Sorry, my brain is in overdrive."

Xavier came over to me and rubbed my arms.

"I get it. But hey, we got this."

"You're right. You ready to go?"

"Yes ma'am. I sent Bruce and his people to the park earlier to scope things out."

We agreed that we didn't want to risk taking the car and ending up on some street surveillance footage. Just in case things were to go awry tonight. Good thing we were extra speedy now. We weren't movie screen vampire fast or anything, but we could get the job done quickly.

The park was fairly close. No need to try to be extra sneaky. Martin knew where Xavier's house was. He could show up at any time. We started our jog over. It was late enough that no one was out and around. Running as fast as we could would definitely raise suspicion. Even though all was quiet, we still stuck to the pig trails when we could.

As we neared the park, we showed our pace. We were a few minutes early and as far as we could tell, Martin had not arrived yet. Our eyes scanned the area looking for threats. We both focused hard on utilizing all of our search. It was something we had been practicing. Honing our skills. We wouldn't understand the full potential of our power otherwise.

"He is here." Xavier said quietly and my heart immediately began to race."

I couldn't see him yet. Xavier must've smelled. He had known Martin for a lot of years. He was more acquainted with his scent than I was. Pretty soon I saw him walking toward a bench positioned under a grove of trees. I exhaled slowly as we made our approach.

"I didn't know that you were bringing your little bitch with you."

"You should have known that she would be with me. I wouldn't leave her side after the little stunt you and Alex pulled."

"Why are we here Xavier?"

"Because the best I can tell, you have devoted your life to destroying mine because you think I killed your daughter."

I typically didn't feel much of an aura from anyone other than Xavier. Right now, I could feel Martin's and it was red hot.

"Maggie was the most precious thing on this earth and you destroyed it."

"You didn't even know who she really was. You were never there!"

"She was a smart girl. A cheerleader. A shining star that burned out to quickly."

"She was a slut. A cheater. The single most shallow person I have ever known. Her stellar schoolwork? I did all of it for her. If you were really part of her life, you would have known that she was not capable of such grades."

"You'd better watch your mouth. You think she was such dirt? Thought you were too good for my Maggie? So what? You molest her… impregnate her… leave her for dead on the side of the road?"

"Impregnate? You are out of your mind. I never slept with Maggie."

"Then why did the cops arrest you? If you were so damn innocent, why did you change your name when you left town? I read the police file. Don't bullshit a bullshitter son."

Arrested? He told me about Maggie, but none of what Martin was mentioning. My head began to spin a little.

"They let me go. Don't you think if I was a killer I would have been tried for something?"

"I think you were careful to leave no DNA behind and you split before they could make anything stick."

"I'm very well-known now and the police were

very aware of my name change. Don't you think they would have come for me by now? They aren't stupid. They know where to find me."

"Says the man with all of the money in the world to beat such a charge. That would be a lot of resources for the taxpayers to waste."

"Sounds like you came prepared with a briefcase full of excuses. Please allow me to tell you what happened that night."

Xavier sounded so callous. It's not at all what I expected. I thought I would hear a wrongfully accused man pleading his case. I didn't know how to interpret so much disdain.

"I showed up to Maggie's house just after sundown. She had a big paper due and as usual; she had not even attempted to do any of the work. So, I quickly wrote the whole thing as soon as I got here because I had bigger plans.

You see, we had an arrangement, I did her schoolwork for her and in return, she let me conduct experiments on her. Don't jump to any conclusions. It was never anything too dangerous. Anyway, she had been getting more demanding but not making a bit of effort herself. She didn't appreciate any of it either. So yes, I felt like she owed me.

If I wasn't busy being her secret helper, she

ignored me. Except for when she joined in when I was getting bullied at school. When I so desperately needed a kind word, she offered vitriol.

I had been developing a pheromone experiment. If it worked, I could turn things around. Maybe I would have an ally. Maybe I could lose my virginity in the process. It didn't work. She laughed at me. I was humiliated. So, I lashed out. I told her what a lazy, selfish, cold-hearted bitch she was. I told her that her life would amount to nothing. She'd be stripping when she was forty so she could feed her car full of illegitimate children. I was done with our arrangement.

I stormed out. I walked from her house all the way to my dad's cabin in the woods. She tried to follow me. She kept yelling... begging me to come back. Without my help, she couldn't pass her classes and it would take her too much time to find another stooge. I never turned back and she eventually gave up.

That was the last time I ever saw her."

Nobody spoke for a few minutes. Even in the silence, the tension was thick.

"That story matched up with what you told the cops. It could be rehearsed though."

After this many years? Come on Martin."

"What is your goal here Xavier?"

"A truce. I am not the monster that you think I am. Can we agree to just go our separate ways?"

"I want to see Alex before I agree to anything. Bring him to me tomorrow night."

"Why?"

"I don't owe you an explanation."

"Fine. Here?"

"No. My new house. I'm sure she remembers the place." He winked at me and my skin crawled.

"Why are you asking me for a meeting with your goon? Call him yourself."

"Because, old friend, I know he is at your house. You seem to have an affinity for sheltering victims. Maybe you should open a shelter." He stood up and began to walk. "Good night."

CHAPTER TWENTY–FOUR

"Hell no. What does he want with me?"

"I don't know. He wouldn't tell me."

"He probably wants to kill me."

"Unfortunately, this is the only way any of us can move forward."

"You promised to protect me."

"And I intend to keep that promise. I said a meeting not an execution."

"I hope you aren't setting me up."

"This isn't a setup Alex."

"When?"

"Tomorrow night."

"Just Martin and me?"

"Amy and I will be there as well."

"We gonna do this in public?"

"Unfortunately, no." Xavier hesitated. "We will be returning to the house you were keeping Amy in. I assume you remember how to ger there."

"I do."

"We will come get you at eight."

Alex nodded and sighed. Xavier and I turned around and headed to our room. Even though he wouldn't be able to hear us through the reinforced walls, we stayed silent until we were back upstairs.

"What do you think we are walking into tomorrow?"

"I wish I knew."

"Maybe he wants to kill Alex. He betrayed him. After tonight Martin knows that Alex must have mentioned Maggie. How else would I have figured it out?"

"Do you think he knows that we are immortal?"

"I don't know. I keep wondering about that

myself. I hope not. He should be smart enough to make such an assumption. Dix Alex seem surprised when you told him?"

I took a moment to think about it. There were so many things going on at the time. The moment didn't particularly stick out in my head.

"He seemed too concerned about other things to dwell on it. Looking back on it, I would have expected a bigger reaction."

"Then I think we should continue this mission with the assumption that yes, he knows about us."

"He might not risk an attack then. Maybe he will think it would be futile."

"Perhaps. As far as I know, he doesn't know what our immortality entails. However, if he had been sneaking around too much. He could have found some of the information."

"Let's hope for the best then."

"I know we should use this time to prepare, but right now I just want to enjoy you. Do you want to take a shower with me?"

I still hadn't said anything about the new details in the Maggie story. It was bothering me. Right now though, I just wanted to forget everything."

"I'd love to."

Xavier took my hand and led me to the

bathroom. He turned the shower on and as steam began to fill the room, he undressed me. In that moment, I felt so small and vulnerable. After trying to be tough in a crappy situation. It was exactly what I needed.

"Just relax." He said softly once we stepped into the shower.

I did as he said and just enjoyed the feel of the hot water on my skin. He began to wash my hair and I closed my eyes. He moved his fingers in tiny circles, massaging my scalp. He moved his hands down slowly until he was massaging my shoulders. As he rinsed my hair he kissed my collarbone softly.

I grabbed the soap as I turned around to face him. I started lathering up his shoulders and slowly made my way down his arms and chest. We had been so busy solving problems and putting out fires that we were forgetting to take time for us.

"Slow down baby or we won't even make it to the bedroom."

I giggled and Xavier began to rinse off. He turned the water off and before I made it out he picked me up. I was straddling his waist and he was grinning at me. There was something feral in his smile and I kind of liked it.

He tossed me onto the bed and was on me before I had a chance to react. Something about the edginess… the masculinity… it excited me. He made me feel safe like nothing could get me here, but I kind of wanted someone to try just so he could stop it.

"I love you, Amy."

"I love you, Xavier." I gasped and I swear the next thing I saw was stars.

When we awoke the next morning, I couldn't help but think about the moments of the night before. From the looks of it, neither could he.

"Good morning, tiger." I said as I rolled over onto my stomach.

"Good morning." He said with a smile.

"Thanks for a magical night."

"The pleasure was all mine I assure you."

"Want some breakfast?"

"I'd love some. I'm starving."

I was happy to oblige. I woke up completely famished. I needed two things: coffee and protein. I scurried to the kitchen and got to work. Once the smell of Colombia's finest began wafting through the house, mom walked into the kitchen.

"Good morning, sweetheart."

"Morning. Breakfast will be ready soon."

I threw sausage and bacon on the griddle. Once

I flipped it, I cracked the eggs and let them fry. By the time food was going onto plates, Xavier walked in. We sat at the table and scarfed our food.

"So, is anyone going to tell me what happened last night?"

I hadn't even thought about it. Once we got home last night, mom went straight to bed. She had to be curious. She was in a relationship with Martin last month.

"It went fine. He wants to see Alex before he will agree to anything." Xavier answered.

"I'm sorry. I should have already told you mom. I didn't think about it."

"Honey it's fine. When will he see Alex?"

"We are bringing him to Martin tonight."

"Please be careful. He might have something up his sleeve."

"Don't worry. I will keep Amy safe." Xavier promised.

"Mom, do you mind staying downstairs again tonight?"

"I don't mind. Better safe than sorry."

"We will be leaving here around eight. Hopefully it won't take long."

"Sounds good." Mom replied before returning

to her meal.

We finished our breakfast in silence. Partially due to our thoughts but also just hunger.

"I was thinking about only working half of the day today. Does that work for everyone?"

"Love it." Mom and I almost said in unison.

Xavier chuckled. "Let's get to it then."

CHAPTER TWENTY-FIVE

The workday passed by quickly. Even faster than a half day usually does.

"I know we need to eat well when we get home so we can be in optimal shape tonight, but my nerves are out of control. I don't know if I can or not."

Once again I spend the drive home talking incessantly. Like I just announced, I was nervous. Who knew what Martin's angle might be? For all we knew, this was planned all along and Alex was just a decoy playing a part.

"Everything will be fine." Xavier said calmly.

I didn't know if he was saying that in response to my conversation or because of the vibes I was putting off. Either way, when we walked into the house fell into our normal routine. Only this time I changed into clothes I could fight in and not pajamas.

Xavier wanted us to do everything we could to feel really charged. Even though we were technically immortal, it was all a bit conditional. For instance, if I was depleted and someone shot me in the head, I would probably die. Xavier was right. We needed to be ready for peak performance.

We started by going outside and soaking up some sun. I don't know if it was the vitamin D or what, but the sunshine always made me feel replenished. While we were out there we did some breathing exercises and stretches too. They served a dual purpose - opening up our minds and getting our bodies ready to fight... or flee.

After we felt satisfied with our results, we went inside. I made us each a strong electrolyte drink and we both gulped it down.

"Well, I guess all that's left is dinner. And a kiss from my beautiful girlfriend."

I stood up on my tiptoes and gave him a kiss.

"What's for dinner?"

"The best fuel for us… meat and fat."

"Steak and eggs?"

"You got it."

"Perfect."

I helped him cook our meal. He grilled the steaks and I made the eggs. I was better at not breaking the yolk than he was, so it had become my job by default.

My previous worries of not being able to eat were long gone as soon as I smelled the steaks. Xavier was working.

"Dinner is served." He said as he walked inside with them.

"Medium rare?"

"Is there any other way?" he grinned as he began making plates.

We enjoyed our meal and tried to be in the moment, not in our won heads. Once we were finished, it was close to eight. We all did the dishes together and mom headed downstairs with us. Sometimes I felt like I was treating her like a prisoner, but it was actually more like precious cargo. Especially after losing my dad.

"Thanks for being such a trooper mom."

"Baby girl, thanks for keeping me safe. Your father would be enormously proud of you."

Her comment filled me with pride and sorrow all at once.

"You ready?" Xavier asked loudly as he opened the door.

"As much as I can be." Alex said solemnly.

Mom walked in and sat down on the couch.

"I'll see you kids soon."

"Love you mama." I said trying not to tear up.

Now wasn't the time to be weak. So, I held my head high and did my best to make my exterior not match my interior.

Once again, we didn't take the car to Martin's house. Alex wasn't prepared for the walk. We kept pace with him, though. No using our extra speed. Even if Alex wasn't lying about being on our side, he didn't need to know what we were capable of.

"One more block." Alex said with what sounded like short, forced breaths.

I didn't recognize my surroundings. In my defense, the last time I was here I was running for my life. I wasn't a very spiritual person, but I was praying. It was a conversation that should have taken place long before now. I could only hope that it wasn't too late."

"Right on time." Martin remarked as we approached his house.

There was no going back now.

"Hey buddy. Long time no see." Martin called to Alex. The smile on his face told me everything I needed to know. Death was on his mind.

"Martin."

"Everyone come in. We have much to discuss."

We hesitantly followed him inside. We all gathered in the kitchen. It was hard not letting my mind go back to the last time I was here.

"We are all gathered here tonight," Martin cleared his voice "because you have all been very bad."

My heart sank to the floor. Just as I feared, we just walked into the lion's den.

"Where should I start?"

The three of us exchanged a quick glance.

"Alex. For years I invested in you. I faked a mentorship. Do you have any idea how much work all of this took? I called you on your shit one time and you decided to flee to Xavier of all people. To be frank, that was quite a bitch move."

"You called me on my shit? You beat the hell out of me dude!"

"A scratch compared to what you have coming. I have no use for a snitch."

Alex didn't say anything else. I couldn't help but wonder why. Maybe he just realized that when you argue with a fool, you have two fools.

"Of course, we all know what my problem is with you Xavier. You talk a strategic game, but I know it was you that killed Maggie. Just because she died doesn't mean we couldn't find out who fathered that baby."

"Martin, for the last time, I did not sleep with Maggie."

"I have no use for liars either."

I was next.

"And as for you, little whore. You have caused me far more trouble than it was worth. Your father was a great man until the end. Your bother was the best soldier that I have ever had. A true comrade. Your mother was a fun toy at best. You though. In my eyes, you're just no longer worth the oxygen you are breathing."

His words stung. And they served their intended purpose because I was too distracted to notice the gun Martin was reaching for. Slow motion activated. I heard the shot. I tried to tap into my speed, but I was frozen. As I braced myself and waited to feel pain, I hoped my body would be able to make it. I could only overcome so much.

No pain.

I opened my eyes and it was like a switch was flipped. Everything was back to normal speed. Nothing was the same as before though. Xavier and Martin were trading punches, knocking each other into the living room. I scanned the room for Alex. It took me a moment to notice him at my feet.

"Alex?"

He was slumped over at my feet. Blood was beginning to pool. Did he take a bullet for me?

"Why did you do that?"

"I owe you a life. I love you, Amy."

This wasn't what I wanted. Not like this. Why should he die some sort of hero? He was an asshole. I stood over him, trembling with anger.

"Amy, you can save me."

"What?"

"Make me immortal. Let me live. I will forever be indebted to you."

I laughed. For a moment, I even felt a bit maniacal.

"You have brought me so much misery. You'll get no sympathy from me." I kicked him as I stepped over him. I refocused my attention on Xavier.

He and Martin were still fighting. Based on Xavier's strength, I thought it would have been an easier fight."

His aura was deteriorating, But why? How?

I moved as fast as I could. I lunged at Martin full force. With my right hand, I hit him over the head with a bottle I grabbed off of the kitchen table on my way through. He fell backward into the entertainment center. Xavier seized the seconds to grab a gun I assumed he hadn't been able to get to."

"Michael." Martin cried."

Xavier shot him in the head. I froze again. My ears were ringing.

"Amy!" Xavier grabbed me by the arms. "We have to go! Now!"

He stared into my eyes and I snapped out of it. I nodded at him quickly and we started running.

Again with the running.

We made it home quickly. There were no sirens. Nothing indicating anyone knew something bad just happened. Still, we needed to remain stealthy and not raise suspicions this evening. We turned out the lights when we entered the house and quietly made our way downstairs. We could shower down here tonight.

"Oh my God. Are you both alright?"

"Yes." Xavier answered sounding more winded than usual.

"The blood isn't ours." I said softly.

Xavier locked the door behind us. We would just hunker down here for the night.

I stood numbly watching the bloody water go down the drain. Why did it have to be like this?

How were we going to clean this up?

Xavier coughed and it snapped me out of my thoughts.

"What's up with you? Something is off." I asked him abruptly.

"I think that asshole drugged me. He stuck me with something but I was never able to see what it was."

"Do you need to go to a doctor?"

"No. If it gets bad enough I will talk to one of the physicians at work tomorrow."

"We are going to work tomorrow?"

"Absolutely. We have to act as if nothing has happened."

"What are we going to do about the bodies?"

"I will send someone to clean it up tomorrow."

"How do we know they won't just turn around and go to the police about it?"

"Because I will be paying a lot of money to ensure that we have no worries."

He was so sure of himself. Seemingly unshaken. Had he done this before?

Michael.

Martin's last word hung around in my head. Why that name? I wanted to ask Xavier, but now wasn't the right time.

We both finished showering and headed for bed. Mom insisted on sleeping on the couch. The room was pitch black. If it weren't for the ambient waterfall tones coming from the sound machine it would have been painfully silent.

"Can we snuggle?"

"I'd love to. I always sleep better when I drift off while holding you. Besides, you know I love being the big spoon."

I slid back in the bed until he was pressed up against my back. It felt safe.

"It's all going to be okay, baby. It might be chaos now, but it won't be forever."

CHAPTER TWENTY-SIX

I jolted out of bed when the alarm went off. It took a moment for me to even figure out why I was sleeping downstairs. Then like a ton of bricks, the events of last night began to replay in my mind.

More death. More souls.

It didn't have to be this way. I was already worried about my soul. Having another death on my hands was not going to help replenish what I might have lost. I might not have pulled the trigger, but I could have saved him. I chose not to. That was on me. I turned my bedside lamp on and Xavier squinted his eyes.

"I feel like shit." He said in a moan.

"You look like it too." I told him as I noticed the dark circles around his eyes.

"Martin really pulled a number on me. I'm going to go splash some cold water on my face."

Xavier got up and walked slowly into the bathroom.

"I'll make us all some breakfast." I yelled out to him as I headed out of the bedroom.

Mom was already awake when I made it into the living area.

"Breakfast upstairs?" I asked as we exchanged good mornings.

"Absolutely."

We walked up together without waiting for Xavier. I knew we needed to talk about last night. As much as I was mentally not ready to talk about it, she deserved to know about Martin's fate. And yet, I hesitated. Maybe not knowing was in her best interest. She obviously noticed that we came home without Alex.

"I'm going to wash up while you cook. We can talk after breakfast if you'd like."

"Ok." I said simply, relieved to be alone.

There was something tugging at me that I couldn't put my finger on. I kept telling myself that it was just because of Alex, but I didn't really believe that. Something was wrong.

"Smells good, babe." Xavier said as he slipped into the room. He seemed to be a bit more refreshed.

"Feeling better?"

"Yes ma'am." He kissed the top of my head. "Where's your mom?"

"Showering. I haven't told her anything yet. I wasn't sure if it was safe for her to know about it."

"We can tell her. The scene is already being dealt with. We should have nothing to worry about."

I was relieved to hear that but troubled at the same time. I needed him to be right about this.

He grabbed plates out of the cabinet for me and I began assembling everyone's food. Mom walked back in right on time.

"Good morning, Xavier."

"Good morning, Joan."

"We are going to work today, I assume."

"That's the plan."

"But there is no need for me to be there

anymore, right?"

"You will always be welcome there."

"I do appreciate that but what I mean, I guess, is that there is no threat for me to hide from. Correct?"

"Yes, that's right."

"Both threats?"

"Yes."

She was silent for a moment. I was so thankful that Xavier was the one having this conversation.

"Well, I'd like to continue my job with the trial patients."

"I think that would be good for them. They all look forward to your visits."

She smiled and we ate our food in silence. Relief was in the air, but something else was hanging there too.

Dread.

I shook it off and excused myself to go get dressed for work. Thankfully, I had the last leg of my surprise project to work on. I needed something else like that to keep me distracted. Otherwise, my mind would wander to places I did not want it to.

When we made it to work, I took a pit stop at Janelle's desk to catch up on her latest escapades. As expected, she had a date with a guy she met on a dating site the night before."

"Oh my gosh! Amy! The guy would not shut up about himself. It was unbelievable. No wonder he was 50 and had never been married."

"50? Dang Janelle. Trying to snag a silver fox?"

"I thought so, but I guess not. It's too much of a difference. In my mind it didn't seem like it would be. There wasn't a lot that we could relate to each other about."

After a bit I excused myself and headed to my office. I grabbed a coffee on the way and sank down in my chair as soon as I got in the room. In the back of my drawer was an emergency candy bar. This morning seemed like a suitable time to sit and enjoy it. Comfort food and all.

Once the chocolate was gone and my coffee started to do its job, I started to get to work. I set an alarm on my phone so I wouldn't get so wrapped up in it that I forgot to see mom for lunch.

I made a lot of good progress. I put my pen down and stretched my arms. All I had left were a few quotes and sources. Xavier was going to be excited about this.

The sound of my door opening startled me and I spun around.

"Sorry. I didn't mean to startle you." Xavier walked in and closed the door behind him.

"It's ok. I was in deep thought. I have an alarm set to meet mom. It hadn't gone off yet. I didn't expect anything to dissuade my focus before then. How's your day going?"

"Pretty shitty. That's why I'm here. I don't even know what to do."

"What's going on?" I gave him my full attention. This seemed serious and the dread that had been looming was now front and center.

"All day I have been trying to figure out what Martin did to me. So, I've been looking at my blood. Toxicology came back negative. Then I looked for broader drugs and deficiencies. Nothing. So, then I took one last sample. I came here as soon as I saw the results. Literally the second I saw them."

"What were you checking for?" I swallowed hard. What was he about to tell me? My heart was racing. I felt my cheeks beginning to flush. My anxiety was now in full effect.

"Amy…" he started, seeming pained to say what was next. "It must have been the antidote."

What?

"Xavier. What are you saying?" I was starting to actually panic now.

"I'm no longer immortal."

I felt like I was just punched in the throat. The only thing I could squeak out was a meager "no."

"Do you want to go home so we can be alone?"

I nodded.

"Why don't you go to the car and I will go get your mom?"

I took his suggestion and headed to the parking lot. It took everything in me not to cry, but I managed to hold it in. As soon as I was in the car, I immediately broke down.

Why couldn't I get a break? He was supposed to be my partner in this. The one person that could navigate eternity with me. Without him I would be alone.

As I sat in the passenger seat of Xavier's car I cried so hard. Why was this happening? It was hard to catch my breath. In an instant, I saw myself hundreds of years from now watching people from afar. Alone.

The doors began to open and it shook me out of my thoughts. Xavier and mom loaded up and we quickly pulled out of the parking lot. I didn't know what explanation Xavier may have given her as to why we were heading home. It didn't matter right now. Nothing did. I felt hopeless.

When we made it to the house, I went straight to the bedroom. I needed some quiet time to gather my thoughts. I was vaguely aware of Xavier trailing not too far behind me. He closed the door quietly behind us and I took a seat on the edge of the bed.

"I will figure this out, Amy. I know what you're thinking. You are not going to be alone."

"The circumstances before just worked. How many times do you think you are going to be close to death? Any me be able to inject you fast enough on top of that?"

"I know it might not seem likely but keep in mind that we have had multiple opportunities arise lately where that could have happened. Unlikely, yes. Impossible, no. Please trust me on this."

I sighed. I wanted him to be right so badly.

"Okay. I will trust you on this. But please Xavier, you have to figure something out. I can't do this on my own."

He kissed the top of my head. I loved it when he did that. It was reassuring. It felt safe.

CHAPTER TWENTY-SEVEN

I looked like hell. You would think that immortality would be a good mask to conceal anything I was feeling. Boy was that wrong. Xavier being normal again was doing a number on my mental health. I felt constantly consumed with the thought of watching everyone I love die and being stuck here alone.

Xavier promised that he would figure things out. I believed him. Still, it was hard not to take any drastic measures. If he was close to death, I could save him. I would be lying if I said that I hadn't thought about bringing him to the brink myself. That was unrealistic, though. If I made any type of misjudgment and he actually died, it would be torture. There was no way I could risk that.

He, on the other hand, was handling everything with such grace. In fact, he was juggling things better now than when he was immortal. I tried not to read too much into that. He was probably just running on pure adrenaline. I know this whole thing had him feeling like a failure. It wasn't his fault. Neither of us expected it to happen.

My mom had gone back to her house. With everything being so turbulent, Xavier hoped that I would ask my mom to stay for a while longer. I know it's what she wanted too but I told her to go. All she would do here is worry about me. She did opt to keep her job at Nectar, which made Xavier very happy. She thought he was just being nice when he told her that she was making a difference with the patients. He meant it, though. Everyone's results were better since she started. All of the scientists agreed that she had an impact on that.

I think the only thing keeping me halfway put together was going to work every day. It forced me to be present and out of my own head for a few hours. I made myself socialize with Janelle. She had to think I was awfully dull these days. I listened to her stories but didn't have a lot to contribute like usual. I felt like a shell of a person. A zombie.

"You ready to go, love?" Xavier appeared at the bathroom door.

"Almost. Trying to look better than I feel." I joked as I finished applying mascara.

"You don't give yourself enough credit. Besides, I told you I think we are close to figuring something out. Just trust me a little."

"I do trust you." I demanded as I made my way out of the bathroom. He followed behind me and closed the door.

He grabbed my arm as I walked into the closet and turned me around.

"I will always take care of you." He pulled me close. "I don't care what it is. I will never stop. So don't get too far into your thoughts because I will be right back on your level. You hear me?"

"Yeah. I know you will. I promise I am trying not to be depressive or mope around. I know that you will figure it out."

I hurriedly finished getting ready for work. I tried not to think about it, but I hoped that Xavier was right. I believed that he would do anything for me. Even if I couldn't feel his frequency anymore. I missed feeling it... our connection. It was something so special. Now that it was gone, a little piece of me felt empty.

He had a cup of coffee ready for me in the car when I finally made it outside.

"Thank you."

"I've got your back." He winked at me and pulled out of the driveway.

I started clicking through the presets on the radio. No good songs to be found. Just lots of morning show chatter. I get the purpose behind the shows. They are probably great for ratings. At some point though, the predictable antics just get annoying.

"Listen, I had an idea for work today."

I turned the volume down and looked at him. What could be up his sleeve?

"Hang out with me. No PR projects or gossip with Janelle. Just me. What do you think?"

"Honestly, I am wondering what you are up to. I trust you, though, so I'm down."

"Thank you. I don't think you will be disappointed."

He was right. As soon as we walked into his office I realized he had already planned all of this. A buffet of delicious looking breakfast foods occupied ceramic trays on his desk. Cinnamon rolls, sausage, mini omelets… it was all of my favorite things.

"You can thank Janelle later. Like I said, you are sticking with me today."

I smiled as I began to munch.

"Are you buttering me up?" I asked with a small mouthful of deliciousness.

"I did think about it coming across that way, but no. I just thought it would be a nice way to start our day together."

"Thank you. It is a great start to the day."

"If I have my way, it is only going to get better from here."

I smiled and he grabbed some food for himself. He started playing music from his phone and we savored our breakfast. We ate until we were stuffed and then we both joked about overindulging.

"Wanna walk some of this off?" Xavier asked me, rubbing his stomach as he stood up.

"No, but it's probably a good idea." I laughed and stuck my hand out for him to help me up.

He took me by the hand and led me out of the office. I didn't ask him any questions about where we were going. I just followed him and tried to solve the mystery in my head. I expected to be going to the clinical trial levels but when we got on the elevator, Xavier chose to do below.

"The immortality level?" I asked quietly. It was

hard not to get excited over why he might be bringing me with him. I wanted to get my hopes up. I didn't want to be let down, either.

"I want to show you something." He smiled at me and there was a twinkle in his eye that I couldn't put my finger on.

When the doors opened, he led me through the maze of a laboratory. We finally made it to the back wall and to a heavy-looking door. He ushered me through it. We were met with a narrow hallway that opened to a larger room. Inside were four very large cages with one mouse inside of each. We walked down to the cage at the very end.

"This little lady is Penelope. She is an extremely healthy mouse. No medical conditions or birth defects. Today, I am going to be injecting her with a serum that is very slightly altered from the original."

"What is different about it?"

"If my calculations are correct, then you don't have to be on the brink of death for the serum to take effect."

"Oh wow." My voice was so quiet I didn't even know if Xavier heard me. My heart was racing. This could be it. I wanted it to be so badly.

"I wanted you to be here for this. I want you to share this with me."

I gave him a hug and choked back a tear. After I let go Xavier pulled a narrow box out of the pocket of his lab coat. When he opened it, I saw a syringe. It was filled with a shimmery blue substance. The original was red. He reached his hand into the cage and the mouse approached him willingly. He slowly held her in place while he injected her. She sniffed around a bit after he released her.

We stood there watching her like someone watching their food cook in the microwave. I don't know what we were expecting to see exactly. Maybe a change in her coat or something.

"How will we know if it has worked or not?" I asked quietly. Before Xavier could answer me though, the mouse suddenly fell over. She was dead. Neither of us said a word but I burst into tears.

"I'm sorry, Amy. I really thought I had it right. I wouldn't have risked it otherwise." He sounded so defeated.

"It's okay. I'm glad you wanted to involve me. I just really wanted it to work."

I caught my breath and Xavier gave me a hug. We stood there for a moment, just holding on to each other. He needed this to work too. It wasn't just me.

"Look at the cage." Xavier said quietly in my

ear.

I turned slowly and looked. Penelope was standing up again, sniffing around her cage. We both inched closer to inspect her. Her coat was a little fuller, shinier. Xavier put a tiny piece of cheese in the far corner of her cage. She smelled it immediately and zipped over to it at record speed.

"Does this mean what I think it does?"

"I can't say for sure yet. We need to try a few things."

"Let's get to it. You have me at your disposal all day and I am ready to dive in."

Xavier chuckled for a minute and then patted me on the butt.

"Let's do it."

CHAPTER TWENTY-EIGHT

I was so disappointed to discover that the kinds of things we needed to check with the mouse couldn't be done in one day. I was ready for results.

"Are you sure this is the fastest way?" I asked Xavier, hoping I wasn't getting on his nerves.

"You realize that this is going to be injected into me, right? I want it to be right. I'm not trying to become a mutant here." He laughed, but I knew he was serious.

"You're right. I'm sorry. I just miss sharing this with you."

"I get it babe."

Xavier had quite the list of things to check. Blood work for I don't know how many things. We had to look at blood, urine, tissue, and cell samples under the microscope. He looked at the hair follicles, teeth health, skin elasticity. You name it, he looked at it.

"I know we are eager, but we need to check these things daily for the next week so we can compare results. After that, we can move forward."

I nodded. It was not as quick as I was hoping for, but it was definitely enough to give me hope.

As promised, I stuck with him for the entire workday. We went to see my mom for lunch like usual. We didn't tell her what was going on in our day, but she could tell we were on to something good. It was hard to hide the mood we were in.

After lunch, we watched a little mouse cardio. He checked off more pages of tests to run. I think that Penelope was just as happy for the workday to be over as we were.

"Wanna stop for dinner?" Xavier asked on our way out.

"You ready my mind. I don't want to cook and it will be a nice little way to celebrate our day."

"Do you wanna pick the place?"

"Nope. Surprise me."

"I figured that's what you would say. Don't

complain if you don't like my choice, though."

"You know what I like."

"Sushi it is then."

I got excited. He knew how much I loved sushi. We didn't eat it very often. Xavier would eat it, but I know he didn't enjoy it. Luckily for him, I found a local restaurant gem. It was all you can eat sushi and Chinese food. Something we both could enjoy.

When we pulled up to the restaurant, I was happy to see a relatively empty parking lot. That meant that the food would be hot and we could relax. As usual, Xavier had already made it to my side of the car when I grabbed my things.

"Always a gentleman." I thanked him as he closed the door behind me.

The host was a young, bubbly girl named Sunni that also ended up being our server and bartender.

"Short staffed tonight?" Xavier asked as she brought us our drinks.

"Yeah. Luckily, business is slow tonight so it's pretty easy to manage. I'll be back in a few minutes for your order."

I spent more time scouring the menu than I needed to while we waited for her to return. I always got the same thing. This place was known for their special roll that was wrapped in soybean paper and deep fried. Yum. Xavier got his usual chicken lo Mein and beef with broccoli. We chit chatted about with Sunni a bit before she skipped back to the kitchen.

"She reminds me of Janelle." I told Xavier and we both laughed.

After a few more rounds of food, we were stuffed and ready to go home. We left Sunni a good tip and wished her a good night. All we talked about on the way home was how stuffed we were and laughed that we couldn't think about anything else. When we made it home, it was a different story. We went to our room and got settled in pretty quickly.

"Are you scared?" I asked Xavier. This whole time I had been thinking about how badly I needed this, I hadn't stopped to think about how he might be feeling.

"Kind of. After I see a few days of consistent results I will start feeling better about it. And for the record, I miss it too. I miss feeling you like that."

"I hope round two is the same as round one."

"Me too. I hope Penelope is okay in the morning."

"She will be. I've got a good feeling about this."

"I like the sudden optimism." He laughed. He had a point. I had been pretty negative lately.

"I'm trying."

We laid there in silence for quite a while. The room was dark.

"Xavier?" I said quietly. Part of me was hoping

that he was asleep already.

"Yeah?"

"You haven't heard anything about Alex or Martin have you?"

"No. It seems like everything was cleaned up nicely. I don't think we have anything to worry about on that front."

I had been waiting for the other shoe to drop this entire time. Having this behind us would be a giant weight lifted.

"Things are going to get better. We are almost through this phase. I don't know what awaits us on the other side of it, but I believe it will be more good than bad."

"Do you feel like you have a soul right now?"

Xavier was noticeably quiet. I almost asked him again, but I decided not to. It was a touchy subject and I was already hesitant to ask.

"I don't really know how to answer that. I feel different than I did before. I don't really remember if it feels the same as before immortality or not. I just know that it is different."

"Did you see or feel anything when you turned back?"

"Nothing that sticks out. I knew something was going on, but that is pretty much the extent of it."

"Sorry for interrogating you. I just have a lot on my mind. Plus, I'm trying to communicate better."

"I promise you, once we are on the same level again, that will be the first thing we tackle. I want the answers as badly as you do."

The thought of whether or not we currently had souls swirled around in my head. I focused hard to shut out everything around me and connect with my soul. I focused harder than I ever had before. Nothing. I felt nothing stirring around inside. I hoped that this was all in my head.

My continued focus did nothing but send me straight to sleep.

CHAPTER TWENTY-NINE

The week had flown by. It was full of research and desperation. Each day ended the same; me obsessing over Penelope's test results. Scanning page after page checking for consistency. Hoping I wouldn't find something that would derail us. It had been exhausting.

We waited until we got home each day to compare the numbers. We could talk more freely there. Not to mention, if we got bad results being at home would be easier. At least I could cry in the comfort of my own home. We decided to be confident on the final day of the week and brought home a vial of the new serum.

"If the test results look good, we can just get this done over the weekend." Xavier said on our ride home from work.

I wanted to jump for joy. That would have been in poor taste. This was a significant risk for Xavier to take. We got lucky with the first serum. Just because that one didn't backfire on either of us didn't mean that would be the case for the second serum. There was a chance that Xavier might not survive. The thought of it made me begin to panic a bit. I hadn't given it much of a thought until now. Perhaps I hadn't wanted to think about it. I was laser focused on what I wanted.

"We can wait longer if you want to. You know, do more tests or try it on another mouse to compare the results?"

"Are you getting cold feet?"

"No, not cold feet. I have just been thinking about the risk. I guess I am scared."

We pulled into the driveway and got out of the car. We didn't say much more as we focused on getting inside and checking out the test results. We spread the paperwork across the coffee table and took a seat on the couch. Piece by piece, we read through the data. There wasn't a piece of ink on that paper that we didn't each read at least twice. The results were perfect.

"This is best case scenario data." Xavier said flatly. It was such a scientist tone.

"It really is. Xavier are you sure that you don't want to try it on at least one more mouse?"

"What are you afraid of, Amy?"

I was quiet for a moment. Truth be told, I didn't even want to put the words that I was thinking out into the universe.

"I'd rather have you be a mortal man for the rest of your life than die this weekend trying to protect me forever." Tears stung my eyes.

It was the truth. This entire time I had been so focused on not being immortal by myself that I didn't think about what kind of life I would have if he died. My mental health couldn't handle any more death. It was already too much.

"If I thought that was going to happen, I wouldn't take the chance. Regardless, I have taken a few extra steps this week. If something bad were to happen, I have made sure that money won't be of any concern to you. You will be fine."

"I don't care about money, Xavier. I care about you."

"I know that. I care about you too. That's why

I want to know you will always be okay, even if I'm not around to see to it."

I leaned over and put my head on his shoulder. He put his arm around me and pulled me in closer. He didn't need to say anything else. This quiet, intimate moment with him was exactly what I needed. I knew that he meant what he said. He would do anything to protect me. I hoped that drive would somehow help the serum work.

"I will let you make the choice. Do you want me to try this tonight or tomorrow?"

"Ugh, I don't want to make this decision. If I had to choose though, I would probably pick tonight. I think if we choose tomorrow all we will do is stress tonight. Why do that to ourselves?"

"I agree with you. I'd prefer to do it tonight. It feels weird planning this out. Last time was so organic. Do you think we should eat dinner first? Do I just go for it?"

"I don't know. A full stomach might make you queasy. I know I am way too nervous to eat right now."

"Good point. I think we should lock up and head downstairs to do this. If we get loud or anything weird happens, it is the safest place to be."

"That makes sense. Let's go put on more

comfortable clothes first."

We walked quietly and closely to the bedroom. I grabbed an old t-shirt and a pair of yoga pants to change into. Xavier picked pajama pants and a white athletic shirt. It was funny to me that he still referred to them as wife beaters. It seemed like a term that someone of his stature wouldn't know about. Either way, he looked sexy wearing it.

"You trying to distract me from my nerves?"

"What?" Xavier chuckled.

"Grey pajama pants and that shirt? If you start doing push-ups or something I'm really gonna get suspicious."

He laughed at me, but still gave me a little wink. I was thankful for the lighthearted moment. It did help my nerves a bit.

"I'm ready when you are." I said to Xavier and I slipped the t-shirt over my head.

"Ready." he said as he walked past me, seizing the opportunity to smack me on the butt.

That was the last thing we said to each other. The second we walked out of our bedroom; my nerves were flying sky high again. Even though I was afraid that I didn't have a soul, I still prayed on our walk downstairs. Hopefully God was still listening out for me.

It was weird walking into the basement. For a second, I expected Alex to be down here. I was glad that he wasn't. Xavier closed the door behind us and we slowly made our way into the dining area.

"Where do you want to do this?" Xavier asked.

"The bedroom I guess. That's probably the most comfortable place down here."

"Sounds good to me. It is a nice mattress."

We made our way into the room and Xavier closed the bedroom door behind us. Normally we would leave it open. Maybe he just wanted an added level of security. Whether he was willing to admit it or not, I knew that he was nervous. How could he not be? I grabbed the remote and found something to put the tv on. I knew we probably wouldn't watch anything, but a little background noise couldn't be a bad thing.

"Good thinking." Xavier said as he sat down on the bed.

"Thanks. I thought it might help." I joined him on the bed. I felt so awkward. I didn't quite know what to do with myself.

"Look, Amy. There's something I want to say before we do this. I just need to get it off of my chest in case I don't get another chance. When I met you, I was an incredibly lonely man. My life was dull and pretty unfulfilled. You changed all of that. The second I saw you walk into that conference room; I was completely captivated by you. Even if I had known that you thought I was a killer, I would have felt the same way. Being with you has been a dream come true. You have shown me a type of love that I didn't even know people were capable of. That love awoke something in me. Something feral. Primal. I promise that I will always love you, protect you, and value you. Hopefully until the end of time. I love you, Amy."

"I love you too, Xavier." I barely managed to choke out.

Before I had a chance to say anything else, Xavier plunged the syringe into leg and pressed the serum in.

"Oh my God!" I exclaimed. I thought we had more time.

We sat there, not moving. Not talking. I was frantically trying to remember what happened when he injected Penelope and how long that took. I couldn't remember. Hopefully Xavier would.

"Hey what happened when Penelo…"

Xavier fell off of the side of the bed. I rushed over to him. He didn't have a pulse. In an instant I remembered what happened when we injected Penelope with the serum.

She died.

CHAPTER THIRTY

"Please just wake up." I cried into Xavier's face.

I don't know how long I had been sitting on the floor beside the bed with Xavier's head in my lap. Cradling him like a hurt puppy. It was long enough for my legs to be numb. His cold face was wet from my tears falling down on him while I hung my head over him.

I didn't know what to do. I couldn't call anyone. If there was someone who could help, he would have told me that beforehand. All I could do was wait and hope. And pray. I closed my eyes as I looked upward, and I just poured my heart out.

"It's Amy again, God. I don't know if you can even hear me. I hope you can. I have lost so many people I love. Please, don't let me lose another one. Not right now. Xavier is a good man. If it weren't for me, he wouldn't have even tried this damn serum. He wants to be here to protect me, though. No matter what the cost is apparently. Please bring him back. Please."

After the third episode of The Office began to play, I became acutely aware of how long I had been sitting here with Xavier in my lap. He still wasn't breathing. He still had no pulse. How long was I going to sit here like this? There wasn't a simple answer to that. I had to have faith that he was going to wake up. He deserved to wake up feeling loved.

I sat there as the fourth episode came on. Soon it would ask me if I was still watching. I wondered what was happening with Xavier. Was any part of his being conscience right now? I checked again for a pulse. Still nothing. His body wasn't as cold as I expected it to be. That had to be a good sign. Maybe something was going on in there that I couldn't see.

The fifth episode started to play. Come on Xavier. I pressed my fingers against his wrist. Still no pulse. His skin was getting warmer. I could feel a spark of hope ignite somewhere inside of me. I sat and stared at him. Desperately searching for any subtle changes. I didn't see anything yet.

I closed my eyes and tried to steady my pulse. Could I feel his frequency? One by one, I closed every other thing out of my mind until the only thing I was focused on was tuning into him. If I could just find the connection. I couldn't feel it. Maybe I was just kidding myself.

Episode six played for a quick second and then paused. It wanted to know if I was still watching. Oh no. The silence was instantly deafening down here. This bunker was so secure that you didn't even hear traffic noise. It was completely silent. The background noise had been more helpful than I realized. I wasn't going to risk going for the remote and Xavier waking up without me.

I sat there and quietly ran my fingers through Xavier's hair. He was such a beautiful man. He was out of my league. He would never agree with that, but I knew it was the truth. I sighed as I watched him, hoping for a little reanimation. I bet back down and kissed him on the forehead. When I sat back up, my lips were tingling. It was almost like hundreds of tiny vibrations. What did it mean?

Still no pulse.

I tried to close everything out and feel for his frequency again. It wasn't working. I thought about how my lips felt after contacting his skin. It gave me an idea, I slid each of my hands inside of his shirt. I waited until my hands were the same temperature as his chest and I closed my eyes again. I focused hard on the areas of contact. Perhaps I could help get it jump started somehow. I stayed zeroed in and soon, something stirred. It was faint, but unmistakable.

I latched on to that feeling. Keep it there. I poured everything I had into a mental tug of war. I was going to grab onto him and pull him back to life. Bit by bit, I pulled him closer. I could feel his body heating up in my lap. Yes.

"Come closer baby. I've got you."

I just kept repeating it over and over. And pulling that feeling closer and closer. My entire body was vibrating. The heat between us got to a point that I was half expecting to burst into flames.

In an instant, Xavier opened his eyes and gasped.

There were so many things I wanted to say, but no words would come out. My tears were free falling now. This was probably a scary image for Xavier to wake up to. My chins. The mascara that must have been all over my face at this point. That poor man.

"You're alive." I finally managed to squeak out.

"I told you I wouldn't risk it if I didn't think it would." He sounded tired.

I bent down and kissed his forehead.

"Do you want to get up on the bed?" I asked, worried if I would even be able to stand myself.

Xavier looked around at his surroundings. I don't think he realized he was laying on the floor until now.

"Yeah. That's probably a good idea."

He sat up slowly and didn't try to stand right away. I used the opportunity to start moving my legs a bit to regain blood flow. Eventually he stood up and extended his hand to help me up.

"Never failing to be a gentleman."

"Never."

We both got up on the bed and got more comfortable. I hit the button on the remote and episode six resumed.

"The background noise helped more than I realized it would." I chuckled.

"How long was I out?"

"Five episodes and about an hour I suppose."

"Wow. That's a lot longer than I would have expected."

"Me too."

"You sat down there the whole time?"

"Of course. I wasn't leaving. I wanted to be the first thing you saw when you opened your eyes. Unfortunately, I didn't think about how much of a hot mess I was going to be."

"You were the most beautiful thing I had ever seen."

I blushed and nestled close to him. I wasn't ready for the hard questions. I just wanted to enjoy the feeling of him for a second. My head against his chest, our frequencies vibrating together… this was my peace.

"Was it different this time?" I asked quietly. Might as well start baby stepping my way into all of the questions I was scared to ask.

"Yes. It was quite different this time." I could hear his heart begin to beat faster.

"Can you tell me about it?"

"Do you remember the first time? Falling through the darkness. Quickly approaching whatever might be waiting at the bottom. Then something suddenly pulls you out? Well, that happened again. However, this time there was more. I know what pulled me out. This time I came back with so much more clarity."

"Well, what was it?" I thought about that

experience every single day since it happened. It occupied so much of my mind.

"It was your soul."

"What?" He knew I was struggling with this. I hope he wasn't making some sort of cute joke.

"It was your soul finding mine. That frequency that we have been feeling. That frequency is our souls. I understand that now. I don't know if it is the serum or just destiny, but we are bound to each other. That's the only reason that the serum worked for me. Amy, if you had left me on that floor to die, that's exactly what would've happened. I am alive right now because of you."

His words hit me hard. He had such certainty in his voice. Something about it assured me that he knew what he was talking about.

"That's why it has hurt so much since you've been mortal."

"I think so too. It makes so much sense to me now. It was easier for me because my senses were so dulled down."

We sat there in silence and episode seven's intro began. My brain felt overloaded. Just quickly trying to process so much information, half of which doesn't make much sense.

"Amy, do you know what this type of

knowledge can bring for us?"

"What do you mean? I thought our plan was to keep the whole immortality thing a secret."

"We are. What I mean is that knowing how souls work, that they actually exist, and each have their own unique frequency… Well, this changes everything."